Samuel French Acting Edition

The Passion of Dracula

A Drama in Three Acts

by Bob Hall & David Richmond

Based on the novel by
Bram Stoker

THE PASSION OF DRACULA was presented by Bob Hall, Eric Krebs and David Richmond at the Cherry Lane Theatre in New York City on September 28, 1977. It was directed by Peter Bennett; the setting was by Bob Hall and Allen Cornell; costumes by Jane Tschetter, and lighting by Allen Cornell. Production Stage Manager: Andrea Naier. The cast, in order of appearance was as follows:

DR. CEDRIC SEWARD .... *K. Lype O'Dell*

JAMESON .... *Brian Bell*

PROFESSOR VAN HELSING .... *Michael Burg*

DR. HELGA VAN ZANDT .... *Alice White*

LORD GODALMING .... *K. C. Wilson*

MR. RENFIELD .... *Elliott Vileen*

WILHELMINA MURRAY .... *Giulia Pagano*

JONATHAN HARKER .... *Samuel Maupin*

COUNT DRACULA .... *Christopher Bernau*

SETTING

England—Autumn 1911
The study of Dr. Seward's home

SYNOPSIS OF SCENES

ACT I

Early Evening

ACT II

Three days later, just past sundown

ACT III

A half-hour later

The Passion of Dracula

ACT ONE

At Rise: *Seward is pacing* u. s. *with a cigar, when something catches his eye at the French doors. He suddenly grabs a gun from the desk and starts to take aim out the doors.*

Seward. (*Opening doors.*) I'll have you this time, you flying barge rat. . . . (Jameson *enters* l. *and crosses to the desk unseen by* Seward.) Damn!

Note: wind blows up each time doors open and out when doors close.

Jameson. (*Crosses up to* Seward.) Dr. Seward (*Startling him.*) —anything wrong?

Seward. (*Points gun at* Jameson, *then relaxes.*) No, Jameson, just tryin' to get a bead on that blasted bat . . . it's been terrifyin' the villagers . . . biggest wingspan I've ever seen . . . (*Sights gun again.*) Flew out of range.

Jameson. Bad luck, sir. You'll have 'im next time . . . is there anything I can get you?

Seward. (*Handing gun to* Jameson, *then crossing to chaise.*) No, thank you, Jameson; you could check on the sanitorium, though. Dr. Van Zandt is still upstairs with Professor Van Helsing . . . don't expect she'll make her usual rounds. (*Sits on chaise.*)

Jameson. (*Returns gun to desk—crosses to* Seward *with clipboard.*) Oh, I've just come from there, sir—

all present and correct. Inmates are on best behavior t'night.

SEWARD. (*Checking clipboard.*) Well, that's a blessing. We've enough to contend with here.

JAMESON. (*Crosses up, closes doors, then crosses back to* SEWARD.) Is the Professor still tryin' to figger out what's ailin' Miss Murray?

SEWARD. (*Giving back clipboard.*) Yes. He and Dr. Van Zandt have been up in her room all this while. I was only in the way, so I cleared off to make room for the specialists . . . (*Rising.*) wish they'd hurry, though. This waitin's too much to bear. (*Crossing* D. L.)

JAMESON. (*Puts clipboard on desk, crosses* D. *to* SEWARD.) Now, sir, you're just overwrought. The Professor only got in from Amsterdam four hours ago.

SEWARD. That all? Feels like an eternity when you're no use . . . y' know, I did fifty battlefield surgeries in two days once during the seige of Mafeking. . . .

JAMESON. (*Having heard the story many times.*) Yes, sir, I remember . . .

SEWARD. . . . and I never once felt so bloody helpless! Gel's wastin' away before m' eyes, and I can't find a cure . . .

JAMESON. Well, if anyone can 'elp it's the Professor. After all, didn't 'e bring 'er through the fever when she was only ten? Now why don't you let me bring you some nice kidney pie and Yorkshire pudding? Can't be gettin' down yourself, y' know . . .

SEWARD. No, thank you, Jameson—perhaps a touch of brandy. (VAN HELSING *enters from stairs.*)

JAMESON. Very good sir. (*Turns* U., *sees* VAN HELSING.) Professor Van Helsing, can I get you a brandy, sir?

VAN HELSING. No, Jameson, thank you. (*Crossing* D. *to* SEWARD. JAMESON *crosses* U. *to bar for brandy.*)

SEWARD. How is she, Abraham?

VAN HELSING. She is resting, poor child. I asked Helga to administer laudanum. Sleep will help her most I think. Cedric, will you go over symptoms one more time? Perhaps now I can make more sense of them.

SEWARD. Well, as I said in my letter, it all started about six weeks ago. I'd have written sooner, but the disease was slow to manifest.

VAN HELSING. She is weakest in the morning, correct?

SEWARD. Yes, a little worse each day. At night she seems to strengthen, but then she lapses into a sort of trance . . . sometimes she even wanders out of the house.

VAN HELSING. You've locked the doors?

SEWARD. Yes, but she keeps finding ways out. It's almost miraculous.

(JAMESON *crosses* D.)

VAN HELSING. (*Stepping* C.) And she remembers nothing of this after?

SEWARD. (*Following* VAN HELSING, *taking brandy snifter from* JAMESON.) No, nothing. Do you have any diagnosis, Abraham?

VAN HELSING. I have common sense. She is exhausted. (*Crosses to fireplace.*) As for diagnosis, I am in the darkness.

SEWARD. (*Crossing* U. C.) But surely there's some test, some laboratory analysis you wish to——

VAN HELSING. Cedric, what tests there are, as good physician, you have performed. What we can learn of her mind, Dr. Helga will tell us with the new techniques of Dr. Sigmund Freud.

JAMESON. (*At desk, dusting.*) 'ere, I've heard of 'im.

Doesn't he claim that little boys have vile notions about their own moth—

SEWARD. (*Cutting him off.*) Jameson . . .

VAN HELSING. Yes, that's the man, Mr. Jameson. It's a fascinating theory.

JAMESON. Shockin' I calls it.

SEWARD. Well, all I know is in the two years since you sent her to me, Helga has done wonders with the patients up on the hill, but this case has her completely baffled. You're the greatest rare-disease man in Europe—if you can't puzzle it out, I don't see any hope.

VAN HELSING. Calmly, Cedric. There is always hope.

SEWARD. I promised old Col. Murray, as he lay dying in the Transvaal, that I'd look after her, and by God, I shall! I love that gel as if she were m' own.

VAN HELSING. We shall cure her, never fear. Now, Mr. Jameson, could you have the carriage readied for me?

JAMESON. Of course, Professor Van Helsing. Shall I drive you?

VAN HELSING. No. No. I drive myself, I find it soothing.

JAMESON. Very good, sir. (JAMESON *exits* L.)

SEWARD. Be careful in town, Abraham. Folk from the sanitorium aren't all that popular these days.

VAN HELSING. I shall be charming Old World Tourist. (HELGA VAN ZANDT *enters from stairs, crosses to* L. C.)

SEWARD. Ah, Helga, how is she?

VAN HELSING. The laudanum has taken effect?

HELGA. (*At desk.*) Finally—she is asleep, poor thing.

SEWARD. That's a mercy.

VAN HELSING. Dr. Van Zandt, Helga, we have not

had time to compare our findings. Your observations, please. (*Stepping* D. C.)

HELGA. Of course, Professor— (*Sits desk chair— opening notebook.*) I have taken copious notes: Beginning on the 14th August, patient manifested severe depression and recited Tennyson for two hours. (SEWARD *and* VAN HELSING *exchange glances.*) At 1:45 p.m. she . . .

VAN HELSING. Capsule summary, please, Doctor. (*Sits on chaise.*)

HELGA. Oh, ja . . . page **49** . . . depression, lethargy and somnambulism, followed by hyperactivity and euphoria. She often rallies and talks incessantly, but this is not unusual in English women of her age. There are symptoms of pernicious aenemia, yet she has a perfectly normal blood count. To me this indicates psychosomatic induction and aberrant manic-depression.

VAN HELSING. I see . . .

SEWARD. (*Edging over to look into* HELGA'S *notes.*) Can't say I do, exactly . . .

VAN HELSING. Is aenemia, but not aenemia, is lethargy and hyperactivity (*Rising.*) . . . very useful, Doctor; (*Crosses* R.) your days in Vienna were not wasted.

HELGA. Ach, danke shön, Herr Professor.

SEWARD. 'Fraid you specialists are just confusin' me. (JAMESON *enters from* L.)

JAMESON. The carriage is out front, Professor. Would you like some coffee before you go?

VAN HELSING. No, thank you, Jameson. (JAMESON *exits* L.)

HELGA. You're going to travel, Professor?

VAN HELSING. To Whitby, to send a cable. I think I shall ask my colleagues to send me a Lazarus wheel.

Seward. A Lazarus wheel?

Van Helsing. A device to induce trance—perhaps mesmerism will prove useful.

Helga. (*Rising.*) I shall ride to the gate with you and walk back. The air will do me good.

Van Helsing. And discuss your diagnosis? (Helga *crosses upright.*) Good night, Cedric, and have courage.

Seward. Take care Abraham. (*Crossing to* Helga.) Somnambulism, and delusions . . . does she discuss her dreams with you?

Helga. Oh, ja, die traume (Helga *precedes* Van Helsing *out* R. *talking as they leave.*) —immer sind sie im farbe. Ich verstehe nicht . . .

Seward. . . . G'bye . . . (*But they are already gone—*Jameson *enters from* L. *with a coffee tray.*)

Jameson. (*After a pause.*) Coffee, sir?

Seward. Hmmm? Oh . . . yes . . . thank you, Jameson. (*Crosses* R., *puts cigar and snifter on mantle.*) Have some yourself if you like.

Jameson. (*At* U. *bar—pours coffee.*) Thank you, sir. Will Lord Godalming be callin' this evening, sir?

Seward. (*Crosses* D. R. *and sits.*) What makes you think he might be, Jameson?

Jameson. Well, sir, he's stopped in every other night for the last several weeks now.

Seward. Yes, he has at that. S'pose as Lord of the Manor he feels a duty to keep an eye on the county . . . and he does worry about us.

Jameson. (*Crosses to* Seward *handing him coffee cup.*) Oh, yes sir. He's devoted to the staff here— (*Sits on chaise facing* Seward.)

Seward. Hem! Jameson . . .

Jameson. Now sir, I wasn't implicatin' no abnormality.

Seward. Should hope not.

JAMESON. I think what he and Dr. Helga do together—

SEWARD. (*Cutting him off.*) JAMESON! (*A small silence.*) Helga said you found Miss Wilhelmina today?

JAMESON. About 5:00 this afternoon, sir. She was standin' by the pool at the end of the hedgerow, starin' vacant-like across the valley. Shouldn't 'ave seen her at all if I hadn't taken the long way up from town.

SEWARD. Oh, of course—the funeral—thoughtless of me. Hope everything went off all right?

JAMESON. Yes sir. Well as could be expected.

SEWARD. Dreadful thing. The girl was your cousin, I believe?

JAMESON. Yes, sir. Oh it did wrench a body's heart . . . little closed white coffin an' all. It'll be a sorry day for the monster what did it when we gets our hands on 'im. Three girls, sir—in the last month—all with their throats torn out. There's some in the village say it's an animal what done it. But I should warn you, sir, there's more say it's a madman.

SEWARD. (*Rising—crossing* L., JAMESON *follows.*) Damn it, Jameson! I know they're talkin' against the sanitorium! You'd think after twenty years . . . (*Puts cup on desk.*)

JAMESON. You know how the men are, sir, give 'em a few pints an' . . .

SEWARD. The stupifyin' ignorance! What do they expect me to do? Chain my patients to the walls? These aren't the Middle Ages any more.

JAMESON. Wull, grief don't mix with reason, sir. An' besides, it's not just us. (HELGA *enters from* R.)

SEWARD. What do you mean, Jameson?

JAMESON. The countryfolk are awfully suspicious of . . . strangers.

HELGA. (*Crossing* D. R.) What strangers did you have in mind, Jameson?

JAMESON. I mean whoever's taken the old abbey. The word is some European fellow moved in six weeks ago, but nobody's ever seen 'im. God only knows what sort he is. (*Crosses* U. *to bar, gets tray.*)

HELGA. (*Crosses* C.—*sits chaise.*) Not only God— I know as well. He is a Transylvanian nobleman, a scholar. He studies English folklore.

SEWARD. Really! How did you discover all this?

HELGA. (*Taking out a cigarette from pocket case.*) I met him last night, walking on the grounds. His name is Dracula—Count Dracula.

JAMESON. (*Crossing* D. C. *in between them.*) 'ere now! What was he doin' on the grounds 'n the first place?

HELGA. Jameson, I think you should confine your concern to inspecting the wards. (JAMESON *looks to* SEWARD, *who nods;* JAMESON *stiffens and starts to exit.*)

JAMESON. Yes'm.

HELGA. And have the attendants keep a special watch on Mr. Renfield.

JAMESON. (*Returning.*) What? Your number one looney? 'e was as good as gold at supper time. No nasty business today.

HELGA. Still, he has been so restless these last few nights, and we cannot be too careful.

JAMESON. Very good, "Doctor." (HELGA *crosses to fireplace.*) Will there be anything else, Dr. Seward?

SEWARD. (*Dismissing him.*) No, thank you, Jameson.

JAMESON. Just ring if you need me, sir. (*He exits* L.)

SEWARD. You say this fellow's name is Dracula? (*Crosses to desk and sits.*)

HELGA. Ja. I've invited him here this evening. He

is a wonderful specimen—I must speak further with him. I trust you will not mind?

SEWARD. What sort of chap is he?

HELGA. (*Lights cigarette.*) I find him fascinating, psychologically. He is arrogant, proud, untempered by the civilization of Western Europe. I confess, I should love to psychoanalyze him.

SEWARD. Well, it's all right with me, so long as it doesn't upset Wilhelmina. (*Rising, crossing* C.) Helga, do you really think the Professor can discover what's wrong with her?

HELGA. I don't know. It's so strange, Cedric. (*Sound of someone beating on the outside door interrupts them.*)

SEWARD. What fool's poundin' on the door in the dead of night?!

GODALMING. (*Off stage.*) Seward, you nit! Are y' in there?

HELGA. Lord Godalming! (*Said excitedly to herself —she primps at the fireplace.*)

SEWARD. (*En route to the door off* R.) I'm comin'! Don't break down m' damn door.

(*Enter* SEWARD *following* GODALMING, *who's in full heat from his ride.*)

GODALMING. (*Crossing* C.) Cedric, you've got trouble. Evenin' Dr. Van Zandt.

HELGA. Lord Godalming.

GODALMING. (*Moving* D. C.) Have y' seen this outrage? (*He produces a soggy newspaper.*) Morning Globe muckrakers are at us again—"mysterious events in Whitby . . . . Village girls murdered and drained of blood . . ."

SEWARD. (*Taking newspaper.*) Well, it's a bit vulgar perhaps, but I don't see . . .

GODALMING. (*Pointing out the paragraph.*) "Whitby, site of Seward sanitorium, where modern experiments in treatment of lunacy are rumored to take place—"

SEWARD. Oh, God— (*Crosses L. to sit at desk—* GODALMING *crosses C.*)

GODALMING. Just so. Goes on like that for half a column. You can bet it's the topic at every pub in the county tomorrow. Journalists! (*Punctuates by hitting his riding crop on the chaise.*) Filthy sensation mongers! Makin' capital out of others' misery! Guttersnipe even had the effrontery to sign it (*Taking paper from* SEWARD.) —some get called Harker . . . Jonathan Harker. Sounds like a poof to me. (*Tosses paper back at* SEWARD.) I'll give Johnny some news if he crosses my path. Fetch me a brandy, will you, Cedric? (*Crosses R. to fireplace.*) I'm beat.

HELGA. (*With a smile.*) I will bring it, my lord. (*Crosses U. to bar.*)

GODALMING. (*In front of fireplace.*) Now look here, Cedric—y' may be a fine doctor, y' may have saved m' life in the Boer War, y' may be my best friend and all, but I can't go on defendin' your damn asylum forever. Bein' lord of the manor doesn't swing the stick it did in the Pater's day.

HELGA. (*Crosses D., hands snifter to* GODALMING.) But my lord this is unwarranted. We have set the highest standards here.

GODALMING. What you have *set*, Dr. Van Zandt, is an absentee record. If one more lunatic goes wanderin' out on his own, the cottagers'll be up here with torches and pitchforks.

HELGA. (*Crossing away to the L.*) Really, Lord Godalming!

GODALMING. Oh, don't protest. I'm aware of your breakaways. That one called Renfield's made a positive career of it.

HELGA. (*Stepping* c.) But we have been so cautious since his last escape . . . he has been in my especial care.

GODALMING. Well much good that's done. P'rhaps Seward should get a man for a man's work.

HELGA. My lord! I should thank you to—! | SEWARD. Uncalled for, Gordon. Not her fault.

GODALMING. Well, I suppose not. Sorry Dr. Van Zandt, but my blood's up. (*Placing snifter on mantle.*) This business could get sticky.

HELGA. (*Crossing* R. *above chaise.*) I assure you every necessary precaution is being taken— (*Loud crash and much commotion from the hall interrupts them.*)

JAMESON. (*Off stage.*) Renfield, you flippin' looney, come back here!

HELGA. Ach! Renfield! | GODALMING.   Hmph. Every necessary precaution . . .

(RENFIELD *runs on from* L. *holding something live and furry in his hands, followed by a panting* JAMESON. RENFIELD *leaps the chaise, scampers* U. R. *but* GODALMING *blocks the exit—then he runs* D. C. *and* JAMESON *grabs him from behind.*)

RENFIELD. (*To* SEWARD *who stands in the* D. S. L. *corner.*) Please, Doctor Seward, don't let him take it, it's mine—mine—mine . . . (RENFIELD *continues fondling the creature saying:* Mine, mine, mine . . . GODALMING *sits on top edge of chaise.*)

JAMESON. Sorry, sir—went to check 'is window an' 'e gave me the slip.

HELGA. (*Beckons* RENFIELD.) Renfield! (JAMESON *shoves* RENFIELD U. C. *to her and stands at* RENFIELD'S L.) What is it in your hand? (RENFIELD *immediately puts both hands behind his back.*)

RENFIELD. Nothing.

HELGA. Show me the hand, Renfield. (RENFIELD *puts out his left hand.*) The other hand, Renfield. (*He returns his left hand and puts out his right.*)

RENFIELD. Nothing.

HELGA. (*Slaps his hand.*) BOTH HANDS, RENFIELD! (RENFIELD *shoves the mouse in her face.*) HELGA *screams and* GODALMING *comforts her.*)

RENFIELD. (*Kneeling* C.—*fondling mouse continuously.*) Dr. Seward, please—it's mine—don't let them take it!

JAMESON. (*Slightly above* RENFIELD.) Field mice, eh? Movin' up in the world, ain't we?

GODALMING. What the devil, Cedric?

SEWARD. It's a symptom, Gordon.

JAMESON. Y' see, M' Lord, he eats creatures.

GODALMING. We all do, man, 'cept G. B. Shaw.

RENFIELD. (*Has been repeating this during the previous speeches.*) Mine—mine—mine—mine—

HELGA. Oh, Enough! (*She grabs the riding crop out of* GODALMING'S *hand and pops the mouse out of* RENFIELD'S *grasp.* It scurries away from under the chaise and* GODALMING *tries to stomp on it as it runs into the wall* D. S. R.)

GODALMING. (*If mouse gets caught.*) Got him! [or]	HELGA. (*If mouse escapes.*) Now it is in the woodwork!

---

*Note: These are alternate lines depending on whether or not Godalming catches the mouse.

JAMESON. (*Fetching a silent butler to scoop up the mouse remains and toss in fireplace if mouse gets caught.*) Y' see? M' lord, live things—flies and such. (*Stepping* C.)

RENFIELD. (*Having watched every movement of the mouse. Animated.*) YES! (*Rising.*) Yes . . . flies, spiders. (*Takes fly out from pouch, crosses to* HELGA *to show it to her.*) Little bits of life, tiny drops of immortality

HELGA. Uh!

RENFIELD. no power in dead things (*Crosses back to* C.) . . . the *blood* is the life!

JAMESON. (*Starting for* RENFIELD.) 'Ere now, Renfield, back you go.

HELGA. (*Stopping him.*) No, no. Let him continue.

RENFIELD. The Master said it and it is so. (*Sits chaise—facing out—holding fly in closed hand.*) Now you . . . (*Indicating the company.*) you eat *dead* things . . . barbarous . . . no life from that—but the living blood still pulsing with the strength, the essence . . . it's glorious!

GODALMING. (*At fireplace.*) So he eats mice?

RENFIELD. No.

GODALMING. Good.

RENFIELD. Flies and spiders. (*Eats fly he's been holding—everyone silently reacts with disdain.*) I was trying to escalate, you see, but it was too soon.

GODALMING. Incredible . . . (*Crosses to doors listening to wolf.*)

(*There is a piercing wolf howl.*)

RENFIELD. (*Transfixed.*) LISTEN—you hear? The Great One rides the wind tonight—the master of life . . . (*Confidentially.*) Oh, I'm not in his league, yet. (*Winks at* HELGA.) I'm a mere journeyman, but soon—soon— (*A chilling scream.* RENFIELD *has a fit—rubbing his head he spins* U. S. C. JAMESON *grabs him from behind and holds him*—HELGA *rises.*) YES! I promise! Renfield keeps your covenant!

SEWARD. (L. *of* RENFIELD *at* C.) Who is this Great One, Renfield?

RENFIELD. Why Him . . . the nameless one.

GODALMING. (R. *of* RENFIELD *above chaise.*) What?

RENFIELD. HIM! . . . But of course you don't understand (*Breaks from* JAMESON *and crosses to* HELGA.) —I speak metaphorically.

HELGA. Of course you do.

RENFIELD. (*Crosses* D. S. *and circles* U. R. SEWARD *motions to the other to protect exits.*) One day the world will know—the philosopher, the scientist, *they* will understand—but you, *you* will never comprehend . . .

(JAMESON *blocks* R. *exit,* HELGA *blocks* L. *exit,* SEWARD *blocks doors. Godalming stands at bar.*)

JAMESON. Steady, Renfield, don't be gettin' in an uproar . . .

RENFIELD. Soon I shall have all the lives I want—

JAMESON. Oh really?!

RENFIELD. the Master has promised me. (*He looks off* R. *as if seeing someone, drawing the others' attention.*) Even now he approaches! (*He grabs* JAMESON'S *eye glasses.*)

JAMESON. 'ere, m' specks . . . !

(RENFIELD *then grabs the riding crop from under* GODALMING'S *arm, bashes* SEWARD *in the leg with it, forcing him away from the doors.* JAMESON *grabs* GODALMING *by mistake.* SEWARD *hops* C.)

RENFIELD. Master, I come! (*And disappears out the French doors.*)

SEWARD. Damn! He's foxed us— (*Limps U. to doors.*)

GODALMING. If he makes the village it's all up for you— (JAMESON *joins* SEWARD *at doors.*)

HELGA. Calmly, gentlemen, calmly! I will fetch lanterns. Cedric, you and Jameson go from the terrace to the ravine; if Lord Godalming and I search the front lawn, we shall close him between us. (*Exit off* L. *for lanterns, coming right back on, placing lanterns on* D. S. *side of desk.*)

SEWARD. (*The riding crop comes flying in thru the doors and* SEWARD *catches it. He gives crop to* GODALMING.) Oh, why didn't I stay in general practice? Come on, Jameson!

JAMESON. Right then we're away. (*They exit through the doors.*)

GODALMING. (*Closes French doors. Crosses* D. R., *leaves crop on chair.*) The things you learn, visitin' other people's houses. (*Turns to* HELGA.) Dr. Van Zandt . . .

HELGA. Lord Godalming . . . (*She rushes into his outstretched arms. They meet at* C. *in front of chaise and sit while still kissing.*)

GODALMING. Ah, Helga, how long must we carry on this subterfuge? Damn Parliament, damn politics, damn Lady Godalming— (*Kneeling.*) run away with me to India, and we'll live like the wanderin' gypsies.

HELGA. (*Embracing him.*) Gordon, you promised. We must conceal a little longer. I should be discredited by every psychologist in Vienna if it were discovered I am the mistress of an English Lord. And you, dear Gordy, you would be ruined in Parliament if the Prime Minister knew of your liaison with an Austrian. The German question is so sensitive. And Lady Doris . . .

GODALMING. Damn Lady Doris!

HELGA. Gordon!

GODALMING. (*Putting his head in her lap.*) Oh, I don't mean it, but it's such agony—she can't live much longer, and she's hated me for years anyway. M' whole life's been a parade dress . . . the family, the title, King and country . . . why can't we have some ordinary peace and happiness?

HELGA. (*Caressing him.*) Because, my lord, we are not ordinary people. We have duties. We are, I'm afraid, hostages to history.

GODALMING. (*Rising.*) Very well, dear doctor, I'll keep m' peace. My God, I wouldn't do this for any other woman in England! (*Bending over her with one knee on the chaise and with one hand on her breast. They embrace and kiss feverishly.*)

SEWARD. (*From off stage.*) Gordon? Helga? Are you there? Where are those lanterns? (*They draw apart as* HELGA *says:*)

HELGA. (*Rising.*) Duty, duty, my dearest lord. (*Crosses* L. *to desk, gets lanterns.*)

GODALMING. (*Picking up crop from chair and crossing* U. S. R.) Off to the front lawn, then, fraulien doctor. Let's go find your prime specimen.

HELGA. The lanterns— (*Crossing to him. They almost kiss, but* SEWARD's *voice interrupts them.*)

SEWARD. (O. S.) Gordon! Helga! (*They exit* R. *The stage is empty for a moment, then* RENFIELD's *head appears at* L. *He enters and giggles softly, crossing* C.)

RENFIELD. Fools—all of them fools. They're gone now, Master. I've distracted them. The way is clear. Now tell me you will fulfill your promise. Teach Renfield the secrets of life. (*The doors blow open, a wolf howls, a wind begins blowing.*)

RENFIELD. (*Listens to the wolf howl, nodding.*) I obey, Master. I will be patient. Thy will be done. (*He exits* L.)

DRACULA. (*Reverberating.*) Wil . . hel . . mina . . . come to me . . . (*And a caped figure appears in profile on the terrace enshrouded in fog.*)

(WILHELMINA MURRAY, *wearing wire rimmed glasses and carrying a copy of* The Dial, *appears on the stairs. She is in a trance, drawn by the voice. Suddenly from the entrance hall we hear:*)

HARKER. (*Poking his head in from* R.) Hello? (*The caped figure vanishes instantly as* HARKER *enters, carrying a camera and various gear. As* DRACULA *disappears* WILLY *stops on the stairs.*) Hello— (*Crossing to the doors as they close when* DRACULA *clears the terrace.*) is anyone in? (*He sees* WILLY.) Oh! Beg pardon, Miss. (WILLY *continues staring vacantly.*) I say . . . Miss? (*Crossing* U. *to her at bottom of stairs. No response.*) Hmm . . . ah, parlez-vous Anglais? Sprechen sie Deutsch? Obviously some sort of trance . . . (*Puts* D. *his carry case, removing cap.*) Well, might as well get a snap for the old *Globe* before I'm chucked out. (HARKER *takes a flash photo. The sudden light startles* WILLY *to consciousness.*)

WILLY. (*Cool and pleasant.*) What are you doing here? Come to that, (*Glancing back upstairs.*) what am I doing here?

HARKER. I just got here.

WILLY. Scavenger hunt, or are you sightseeing?

HARKER. Motorcar's failed. Think it's the dashed magneto. Saw your light through the fog and came up.

WILLY. (*Descending the stairs.*) Motorcar frightfully sporty . . . but wildly improbable! (*Crosses

D. L. *to desk.*) What sort of motorcar? (*Leaves the "Dial" on desk.*)

HARKER. (*Crossing* C.) Borrowed, actually. Who's house am I in, by the bye?

WILLY. (*Turning to him.*) Dr. Cedric Seward's. And who are you, by the bye?

HARKER. (*Puts camera and flash on* C. *table.*) What? Oh, sorry, I'm Jonathan Harker of the *London Globe.*

WILLY. Of course! You're here to serialize my autobiography! (*Offers hand.*)

HARKER. Ah, why, yes, Miss, that's just it . . .

WILLY. (*Giggling.*) Your tone gives you away. (*Crosses* R.) You've just decided I'm an inmate.

HARKER. Inmate? Beg pardon?

WILLY. (*Moving in front of fireplace.*) Dr. Seward is the head of the Whitby Sanitorium.

HARKER. (*Mock astonishment.*) Yes, of course! The great gloomy heap on the hill. I knew it was somewhere in these parts. Are you a—patient?

WILLY. You're the reporter—draw an inference. Any rate, you're welcome. That is if Uncle Cedric doesn't murder you in cold blood—hates the Press.

HARKER. Doesn't everyone?

WILLY. Take off your coat and warm yourself by the fire. (HARKER *removes coat, lays it on chaise meets* WILLY *at* R. *just above fireplace.*) Care for a brandy? Promise you'll be civil and entertaining and I'll intercede for you. I'm Wilhelmina Murray. (*Taking a cigar from the mantle.*) Would you like a cigar?

HARKER. (*Taking cigar.*) Ah . . . charmed, Miss Murray.

WILLY. Call me Willy. (*Offers hand.*) Everyone does, sooner or later.

HARKER. Willy. (*Takes hand and kisses it.*) Call me Jonathan—almost no one does. (*Step aside to let her pass.* WILLY *crosses* U. *to bar for brandy.*) Yes to the brandy, I'm usually civil if softly approached, I almost never smoke cigars (*Chucks away cigar in box on mantle.*) and I promise to be as entertaining as possible. (*Crosses* U *to stair post.*)

WILLY. (*Pouring brandy.*) Capital! You may improve on acquaintance. (*Handing him glass.*) Here's your brandy, I hate cigars, and a writer's promise is a tiger's smile—as Oscar Wilde once said. (*A pause as* HARKER *leans in for a kiss—but* WILLY *crosses* C.) I wonder where everyone is, come to think of it . . .

HARKER. (*Crossing* L. *above* WILLY *to doors.*) Wouldn't have been the lanterns I saw going down the edge of the grounds as I came in?

WILLY. Really? Hmmm, must be chasing the Renfield again.

HARKER. The who?

WILLY. (*Stepping* C.) The local diversion.

HARKER. Proper inmate?

WILLY. Oh, yes. I rather enjoy his escapades . . . lightens the hours. (*Steps* D. C. *removing eyeglasses.*) You've no idea how dull country life can be.

HARKER. (*Moving in to her.*) It needn't be . . .

WILLY. Are you really a reporter, or are you here to filch the heirlooms?

HARKER. (*A slight pause.*) It wasn't Wilde.

WILLY. What?

HARKER. "A writer's promise . . . like a tiger's smile . . ." It wasn't Wilde, it was Lytton Strachey.

WILLY. It reads! Delightful! (*Puts smiling glasses on and crosses* U. C. *to camera.*)

HARKER. (*Puts brandy* D. *on desk and crosses* C.) Well, one tries. Now, if you will, a few explanations. What on earth were you doing when I came in?

WILLY. No interviews, please. How does this work? (*Indicates camera.*)

HARKER. Here I'll show you. Stand over there, will you? (*Indicating French doors.*)

WILLY. (*Crosses to doors.* HARKER *takes camera from table to bar leaving one photoplate on the table.*) Right. Oh, and please excuse my running on—I tend to prattle—left alone as a child. They say it's compulsive.

HARKER. (*Setting up for the photo.*) Certainly. Think nothing of it. Now . . . (*Crosses to her and removes her glasses.*) Hold your head like this . . . chin up . . . (*Touches her cheek. Takes a beat to look at her —puts glasses on bar and crosses back to her.*)

WILLY. . . . and I've had a slight temperature—it's left me a bit giddy.

HARKER. (*Taking her hands.*) Well, fever may have addled your wit, but it's given you a lovely color . . .

WILLY. Smooth-tongued rogue. (HARKER *draws her to him and kisses her.*) Do give me fair warning next time—I hate surprises—was frightened by a grouse hunt as a child.

HARKER. Now, don't move a muscle . . . (*He starts to cross to the camera. The shadow of a bat appears at the French doors and* DRACULA *theme is heard.*)

WILLY. (*Weakly, grabbing his arm.*) Jonathan—

HARKER. Miss Murray—what is it? Are you unwell?

WILLY. . . . do you believe in the intervention of fate?

HARKER. I never did . . . till now . . .

(*The bat swoops the windows again and* WILLY *shudders and swoons.*)

HARKER. (*Supporting her.*) My dear girl—you're

quite in need of some air. Let's step out on the terrace. (HARKER *opens the French doors, supporting* WILLY *with an arm around her waist. Just as they step out the bat swoops again.*)

WILLY. Ahhh— (*She breaks from* HARKER *and backs into the room* D. S. *of the chaise.*)

HARKER. Jesus! Look at the size of that bat! Well, we'll see to this . . . (*He grabs a fire poker and rushes at the bat. In the struggle he's nicked on the forehead,* O. S. *but drives the bat off. He re-enters and closes the doors.*) Things that go bump in the night. Good Lord deliver us. Vicious beast— (*Crosses* C.) damn! He's blooded me— (*Noticing* WILLY, *who is hysterical.*) Miss Murray, Willy, you are unwell . . . (DRACULA *theme goes out.*)

WILLY. (*Wildly.*) It will out, they say—blood will have blood! (*She suddenly recovers her composure.*) Jonathan, come here. (*He takes her hands.*) I'm going to faint, please excuse it. If I die, or go mad, please remember that I liked you very much . . . (*She faints dead away on the chaise.*)

HARKER. (*At* L. *of chaise.*) My dear girl . . . Willy . . . Oh, Christ, her Uncle'll have me flayed alive . . . (*Patting her hand, he is attempting to revive her when* RENFIELD *opens doors and enters then closes doors. Thinking* HARKER *is attempting to harm* WILLY, RENFIELD *grabs him in a bear hug and swings him away from the chaise to* U. S. C. *holding him off the ground.*)

HARKER. Eeeeeaaaaahhhh!

RENFIELD. You're new here, aren't you?

HARKER. WHAT THE—!

RENFIELD. Shush! Quiet now! I'll explain the rules. You must never, never touch Miss Wilhelmina. That's very naughty. She is . . . promised. And you shouldn't be out of your room at all after dark. That's very wrong.

HARKER. Will . . . you . . . please . . . put . . . me . . . down?

RENFIELD. Promise not to run?

HARKER. Cross my heart. (RENFIELD *puts him down and* HARKER *breaks to the* L.) Now look here—there's been some misunderstanding.

RENFIELD. There always is . . .

HARKER. (*Taking one step toward him.*) My good man—what is your name?

RENFIELD. (*Taking one step toward him.*) You first.

HARKER. (*Taking another step in.*) John Harker—and you are . . . ?

RENFIELD. I'm Jameson, the butler here. You'll be seeing a lot of me . . . (*Takes* JAMESON'S *glasses out of his pouch and puts them on. Crosses* D. R. *to* WILLY *and pats her hand.*) . . . we try to make everyone feel at home . . . while they regain their Life Force . . . must care for the Life Force . . . feed it . . . nurture it . . .

HARKER. (*Watching* RENFIELD.) Yes, but . . .

RENFIELD. (*Begins to wander* L., *tracking a fly. It lands on the wall. He steps* U. *onto the stool and catches it, shows the fly to* HARKER *and then eats it.*) Must sustain the Life Force!

HARKER. (*Very softly with a gulp.*) Oh, Lord have mercy on a poor wayfarer . . .

(*General commotion* O. S. R. HARKER *is confused—he looks at* WILLY *then to* RENFIELD *who tries to hide by holding the stool over his head cringing in the* D. S. L. *corner.*)

off-stage

> SEWARD. He must have come this way—doubled back—
> JAMESON. Must 'ave done—
> HELGA. But Gordon—
> SEWARD. *How* could Godalming get lost?
> HELGA. His torch went out, I think—
> SEWARD. Maddening—

(*They all enter.*)

SEWARD. (*Opening the doors.*) But where could Renfield— (*All three stop dead in the doorway when they see* HARKER. *Looking at them* HARKER *simply points to where* RENFIELD *has hidden—they all look toward* RENFIELD *simultaneously.*)

SEWARD. (HELGA *closes the doors, puts down her lantern, crosses to* WILLY *at* L. *of chaise checking her pulse.*) Right . . . Jameson . . . (JAMESON *bounds across the room and collars* RENFIELD, *retrieves his glasses, puts the stool down and sits* RENFIELD *in the desk chair.*)

HARKER. (*Indicating* WILLY *and crossing* D. S. R.) . . . and your niece, I think, has fainted.

SEWARD. (*Crossing* R., *kneeling at* WILLY'S *side.*) Willy! What's happened here—and WHO IN HELL ARE YOU?

HARKER. I'm John Harker, reporter—your niece was frightened by a bat and fainted when that fellow came in and grabbed me . . .

SEWARD. Young man, I'll . . .

WILLY. (*Revives and sits up.*) What is the deed without a name? . . . up above the world so high, like a tea-tray in the sky (*Pause.*) . . . Hello, everyone . . . what? . . . Oh, Lord, I've nodded off again.

My apologies, Mr. Harker. I seem to be subject to fits these days.

SEWARD. Thank God you're all right! (*Rising.*) Now see here, Harker . . .

WILLY. Uncle, Please . . . Mr. Harker's a—motorist in distress. He saved me from—well, probably rabies at the least—now be civil! I'm sure he'll refrain from writing about us if we're hospitable—

(*During this exchange,* RENFIELD *has picked up the poker that* HARKER *dropped on the floor near the desk.* HELGA *notices and quietly looks at* JAMESON, *points to* RENFIELD. JAMESON *takes the poker from* RENFIELD.)

HARKER. My word as an Oxford man.

SEWARD. Humph. Which House?

HARKER. Magdalen, sir. (*Pronounced: Maudlin.*)

SEWARD. Corpus Christi, m'self. How'd ja do?

HARKER. (*Shaking* SEWARD's *hand.*) Pleased to meet you, sir.

WILLY. (*Rising, crosses into* HARKER *in front of* SEWARD.) Glad that's settled! What's an Oxford man doing reporting?

HARKER. Yes . . . family's frightfully cut up about it—

SEWARD. (*Crossing* L. *above* RENFIELD.) Everything all right, Jameson? (RENFIELD *begins rocking and rubbing his head, swinging into a manic phase.*)

RENFIELD. (*Rising.*) He . . . he . . . he cometh, he cometh . . . (*He advances* C. *towards* WILLY. JAMESON *puts the poker on the desk.*) He comes to judge the quick and the dead—

WILLY. (*Stepping to him.*) Who, Renfield?

RENFIELD. Ye have eyes, and ye see not, ears and ye hear not . . . Fools! Fools, more than fools (*He leaps onto the chaise.*) . . . Food! Hahahehehe . . .

WILLY. (JAMESON *starts for* RENFIELD *but* HELGA *stops him.*) You don't mean that, Renfield—

RENFIELD. Yes, yes, I do . . . all, except you.

WILLY. Why do you say that?

RENFIELD. I . . . I . . . can't tell . . . (*In great agitation.*)

WILLY. (*Taking his hands.*) You can tell me, Renfield—why am I the exception?

RENFIELD. Because—you are chosen! (*He jumps off the chaise, still holding* WILLY's *hands.*) I told him, you see . . . I told him how you were special . . . I've always thought you were . . . (*Letting go of her wincing in pain.*) Noooo! (HARKER *draws* WILLY R.— *away from* RENFIELD.) No, Master! I wouldn't tell them—never! I didn't mean to— Don't punish me, please!

SEWARD. Jameson!

RENFIELD. (*As* JAMESON *crosses* C. *and puts his hands on* RENFIELD's *shoulders:*) No! Don't touch me! Stay away from me— (*He pushes* JAMESON *away. General ad-libs to calm* RENFIELD. HARKER, SEWARD *and* JAMESON *start for him and surround him. To the* R. JAMESON *coming at him from* D. S. *He drops to his knees, grabs the poker from desk, swings at them and knocks the gun out of* JAMESON's *hand screaming: the gun flies* S. R.—JAMESON *goes after it to the fireplace everyone focuses on* RENFIELD *as he backs* D. S. *watching him sink to his knees—*HELGA *is* U. S. L., SEWARD *and* HARKER *are* U. S. R. JAMESON *is at the fireplace,* WILLY *is extreme corner* D. S. R.) BACK! (*Suddenly* RENFIELD *turns and bolts for the French doors . . . just as suddenly he stops,* DRACULA *theme is heard*

. . . *backs up saying:*) The blood is the life . . . the blood is the life . . . (WILLY *has trouble breathing totally affected by* DRACULA's *approach. He is in great agitation. Trembling, he collapses onto the floor. The doors swing open, wind blows and* DRACULA *steps into the room to the edge of the first platform.*)

JAMESON. Lord!
HELGA. Mein Gott!   (*Together as soon as doors open.*)
HARKER. What now?

DRACULA. (*Pausing to look at everyone before speaking.*) Good evening . . . I am Dracula.

SEWARD. Sir?

DRACULA. Count Dracula, late of Transylvania. As I approached, I heard the sounds of struggle.

SEWARD. Well, you certainly seem to have come just in time.

HARKER. You rather surprised us, Count.

SEWARD. Yes . . . well . . . we'd best get him back to his cell— (*Indicating* RENFIELD.)

JAMESON. I'll need some 'elp, sir. (HARKER *offers to assist but before they can move:*)

DRACULA. One moment. (*He crosses* D. S. C. *to* RENFIELD *who has begun to whimper and moan.* DRACULA *with one quick movement reaches out and with his upstage hand he presses his finger tips to* RENFIELD's *forehead and* RENFIELD *rises slowly, completely subdued.* DRACULA *removes his hand and wipes it with his handkerchief.*) He will go with you now.

JAMESON. (*Crossing* D. C.) If you say so, sir (*Picking up poker.*) . . . After you, Renfield. (RENFIELD, *in somewhat of a daze, precedes* JAMESON *down the hall exiting* L. *As they exit,* DRACULA *counters* U. *to* C. SEWARD *crosses* L. *and closes doors.*)

HELGA. (U. S. *of desk.*) Amazing, Mein Herr, remarkable effect you have on the Renfield.

DRACULA. In my family there are certain gifts . . . to quiet . . . to heal.

HARKER. Indeed.

DRACULA. Yes, my house is an ancient one. We are descended from the Hun. The blood of Attila flows in these veins. (*He gazes at* WILLY.)

HELGA. (*Sitting in desk chair.*) But this is fascinating, Count. You must speak further . . .

DRACULA. But I fear the company have rather the advantage of me.

SEWARD. (*Stepping* D. *to* DRACULA'S L.) Oh, silly of me. I believe you know Dr. Van Zandt; this is Jonathan Harker; I'm Cedric Seward; and this is my niece, Wilhelmina Murray. (DRACULA *nods to* HELGA, *bows to* HARKER *and* SEWARD, *crosses* D. R. *to* WILLY, *who takes a step into* C. WILLY *starts to curtsy but* DRACULA *reaches for her hand and kisses it. When* DRACULA *crosses to* WILLY, SEWARD *and* HARKER *counter* C. *above chaise.*)

DRACULA. Charmed, Miss Murray.

WILLY. I . . . I feel almost as if we had met before . . .

DRACULA. Perhaps in a dream . . . (*He smiles.*)

WILLY. Are you long in this country, Count?

DRACULA. Alas, no. My business here concludes itself within the fortnight; but I could not resist the chance to meet my charming neighbours face to face just once.

WILLY. Only once? You must give us the chance to know you better.

DRACULA. Ah, but to know you, Miss Murray, I feel, would take a lifetime . . . perhaps . . . several . . . lifetimes . . . (*Another smile.*)

HARKER. (*Crossing* D. C.) And you're only here for a few days—pity. Are you travellin' for pleasure, Count?

DRACULA. I take pleasure in those I meet along the

way . . . and from walking on occasion in the company of men . . .

HARKER. You're sayin' you spend a lot of time alone, then, Count?

DRACULA. (*Practically cutting him off which sends* HARKER *back up to* C.) My native land has grown barren you see. There are few of us left. I, myself, am the last of my line.

HELGA. The very last? How that must prey upon your mind . . . (*This turns* DRACULA *to stare at her, making her uncomfortable.*)

SEWARD. I say, Harker, your forehead's bleedin'.

HARKER. What? Oh, yes, where that damn bat nicked me.

DRACULA. (*Crossing* U. R. *to* HARKER *above chaise.*) A bat? Take care, Mr. Harker—such a wound can be more dangerous than you think . . . (*Slight pause, then* HARKER *crosses* U. *to doors.*)

VAN HELSING. (*From* D. *the front hall.*) Cedric . . . Cedric . . . Where is anybody? (*He enters from* R. SEWARD *crosses* U. R. *to meet* VAN HELSING, DRACULA *crosses* C. *to stare at* HELGA. WILLY *moves back to the far* D. S. R. *corner.*)

SEWARD. Hello, Abraham. (SEWARD *motions to* WILLY *to make introductions.*)

VAN HELSING. Hello . . . you have guests. (*Crossing* D. R. *to her.*) Willy! What are you doing out of bed?

WILLY. It's been a very busy night. Don't worry, I feel much better now. (*Kisses him on the cheek.*) Ah, Professor Abraham Van Helsing, (*The mention of* VAN HELSING's *name turns* DRACULA *to him.*) this is Jonathan Harker—

VAN HELSING. Good evening, Mr. Harker.

HARKER. (*Crossing* R. *to* VAN HELSING.) Professor . . . (*Shakes his hand.*)

WILLY. . . . and Count Dracula.

VAN HELSING. (*Stepping in, so that there is a clear visual line between* VAN HELSING *and* DRACULA.) Count . . .

DRACULA. Drac . . u . . la—

VAN HELSING. Yes, that name is familiar to me, I think . . .

DRACULA. And yours to me. I have read your works.

VAN HELSING. Really?

DRACULA. With great pleasure.

VAN HELSING. . . . of course! I mention one of your ancestors—the hero of the Turkish wars.

DRACULA. The same: Vlad Dracula. He is a legend among my people.

VAN HELSING. And among the Turks as well. Though they had another name for him—

DRACULA. Yes, Vlad the Impaler. Those were barbarous times. He was cruel, but just. No doubt Professor, your studies revealed the many calumnies his memory endured?

WILLY. (*Crossing to* DRACULA *at his left.*) He was slandered?

VAN HELSING. Perhaps the Count would rather not . . .

DRACULA. No, no. These tales amuse me. You will think I invent, Miss Murray, but Vlad Dracula was said to be—

VAN HELSING. (*Coming right in—finishing the sentence. A dawning suspicion.*) —a vampire . . .

WILLY. How thrilling! (*A loud wolf howl is heard very near.*)

HELGA. (*Rising.*) Please excuse me everyone—Lord Godalming comes not yet back. (*Crossing* U. *to doors.*)

I think I should go to thé end of the terrace. (*Opens doors.*)

SEWARD. Quite right, Helga. Best I go with you. (*Picks up lantern, crosses to doors.*) Please excuse me gentlemen, I have another guest lost out on the lawn. (HELGA *exits.*)

VAN HELSING. (*Following* SEWARD *to doors.*) Cedric, there is some trouble?

SEWARD. No, it's just Gordy . . . (*He exits.* VAN HELSING *closes the doors.*)

WILLY. (*Sitting in desk chair.*) Do tell us more, Count.

DRACULA. (*At* c.) I fear these gentlemen will laugh at the superstitions of my backward country.

VAN HELSING. (*Crossing* D. *to stand above* WILLY *at* U. S. L.) No, no, is facinating. Tell us of your ancestor the vampire . . .

HARKER. (*Stepping* c.) Indeed . . .

WILLY. Shhh. (*Having been dismissed,* HARKER *retreats and sits in the* U. S. R. *chair.*)

DRACULA. (*Focusing on* WILLY.) The peasants said that he drank the blood of his captives, and thus gained immortality. Such legends persist to this day.

VAN HELSING. Is it not said that the vampire can be killed only by a stake driven through the heart?

DRACULA. Just so.

VAN HELSING. And are they not said to be shape-shifters?

DRACULA. To change into beasts at will? It is said of magicians . . . they tell this of your King Arthur's Merlin, do they not?

VAN HELSING. And do they not fear the articles of Christian faith? . . . the Host, the holy water . . . and . . . (*He picks up a Bible from the desk with a silver cross embossed on the cover and holds it toward* DRACULA.) . . . the cross?

DRACULA. (*They gaze at each other—there is a moment of recognition.*) The parish priests would have it so. (DRACULA *crosses away from* VAN HELSING *to the* D. S. R. *corner.*)

VAN HELSING. (*A pause as* DRACULA *turns and looks at him.*) No myth but has some grain of truth . . . I think . . . (*Another pause.*)

HARKER. (*Rising—crosses to* C.) Vampires . . . blood sucking beasts! Incredible, really, how a story grows in the telling—

DRACULA. (*Facing out.*) The lore of my poor country seems ridiculous, Mr. Harker?

HARKER. It's just that the whole idea is so . . . alien to the twentieth century.

DRACULA. I wish not to be an object of mirth. (*After the line he fixes his gaze on* HARKER.)

HARKER. (*Uncomfortably.*) Pardon me, Count— (*Crosses* L. *to bar to get camera ready—second flash device having been pre-set on bar.*)

DRACULA. (*Crossing in front of fireplace.*) Ah, my pride is at fault . . . a retiring scholar from a faraway land . . . I am not at ease in company, I fear, having spent so long in study.

VAN HELSING. And you study . . . ?

DRACULA. (*A smile.*) The nature of . . . life . . . (HARKER *has drifted to his camera, turns suddenly and takes a shot of* DRACULA, *who is enraged, but controls himself.*)

HARKER. (*Pulls the second plate from camera, retrieves the first from the* C. *table holding both in one hand the camera in the other.*) Didn't mean to startle you, Count, but I thought to have another snap to commemorate the occasion.

DRACULA. (*Advancing* U. *to* HARKER *at* C. *With dreadful calm.*) In my country we keep the ancient teaching and make no graven images.

HARKER. (*Backing off to exit of* C.) Dreadfully sorry —meant no harm.

VAN HELSING. (*Who has been watching carefully crossing* U. *to* HARKER.) Mr. Harker meant not to offend your religious views, Count, I am sure. How if we purify elementally? (*Having crossed to* HARKER *he takes the photoplate of* WILLY *from him.* HARKER *thinks that* VAN HELSING *has made a mistake and starts to protest:*)

HARKER. Professor, that's not . . .

VAN HELSING. (*Crosses to the fireplace.*) That's not to worry, my boy. (*Flings photoplate into it.*) There! We have resolve cultural difference!

HARKER. Well, that's what counts, Count. I do apologize.

DRACULA. (*Having watched closely.*) Think no more of it.

WILLY. (*Rising.*) Count, where did you say you were staying?

(VAN HELSING *and* HARKER *have a silent exchange about the plate.* HARKER *holds the second plate behind his back, at* U. S. R.)

DRACULA. (*Crossing* C. *to her.*) For now I have taken the Castle Carfax, across your charming valley.

WILLY. But isn't it practically in ruins?

DRACULA. Yes, but it will serve. And it reminds me of my homeland, alas.

WILLY. You sound so sad.

DRACULA. I think of my country in more glorious times. Now a poor, cruel land . . . but the winds that blow cold across my battlements will welcome me. There I shall not be the foreigner.

(Wolf howls are heard in the distance.)

SEWARD. *(Opening doors entering from the terrace crosses C. next to* HARKER.*)* Damn beasties! Wonder what sets 'em off . . .

DRACULA. *(Facing out.)* They sing the music of olden times, when man was one with the creatures of the night. In my country we still hear the song, though we may not know the words. Ah, but I tire you with reminiscences. *(To* WILLY.*)* Allow me to take my leave, my . . . pleasant . . . neighbours. *(Taking* WILLY's *hand, he turns it over and kisses her up-turned wrist; he steps C.—bows to everyone then crosses to the French doors.)*

VAN HELSING. Perhaps we shall meet again.

DRACULA. *(Halting in the doorway.)* Depend upon it. *(With a wry smile he is gone.)*

SEWARD. Hmph. Abrupt fellow.

WILLY. *(Crossing to doors, looking after* DRACULA.*)* Strange man . . .

VAN HELSING. *(Calling.)* Helga! *(Stepping U. R., taking photoplate from* HARKER.*)* Mr. Harker, you have chemicals to develop photograph?

HARKER. Why, yes, but . . .

VAN HELSING. Good! Bring them! HELGA!

HELGA. *(Entering from the terrace with lantern.)* Ja, ja, vas ist?

VAN HELSING. Ja, ja. Stay with Willy—do not leave her.

SEWARD. But what . . .

VAN HELSING. COME! *(Carrying the photo slides he rushes up stairs. The others look perplexed and fol-*

low. HARKER *taking all of his camera equipment—* SEWARD *follows.)*

HELGA. *(Closes doors and crosses* D. L. *putting lantern on desk.)* What possesses the Professor?

WILLY. *(Stepping* C.*)* I'm sure I don't know. The Count left, and he started commandeering everybody. *(Pause.)* What did you think of the Count?

HELGA. I should love to study him at close range.

WILLY. I should think. Helga, I realize I'm under house arrest, but could you get me my copy of *The Dial?* I think it's on the night table. I promise not to have a fit until your return.

HELGA. *(Crossing to* WILLY.*)* Very well. Try to rest, Wilhelmina. *(A beat as they look at each other. Then* HELGA *exits up the stairs as we hear the sinister* DRACULA *theme.* WILLY *stands* C. *staring at her wrist facing out and* DRACULA *appears through the doors, crosses silently down to* WILLY.*)*

DRACULA. *(Startling her, she turns to him.)* Miss Murray.

WILLY. Why, Count! I thought you had left us forever.

DRACULA. I was rude in my leavetaking, I fear, and I very much desire your good opinion, dear lady.

WILLY. And it is yours, of course. But, it is I who am socially remiss. Can I offer you a sherry? Some brandy?

DRACULA. I never drink wine. *(Pause.)* Tonight, dear lady, I drink of your beauty and am content.

WILLY. Why, Count! If it weren't for my silly malady, I think I should blush.

DRACULA. Ah, forgive me . . . I tire you with my attentions . . . you should rest . . . *(A long pause as he puts her in a trance, smiles, then he crosses* U. S. *to the French doors.)*

WILLY. Count, (DRACULA *stops just inside the doors. She crosses in front of him at the doors.*) What do you see, out there in the fog?

DRACULA. Destiny . . . (*The spell begins. He gently caresses her shoulders and draws her to him.*) Wil . . hel . . min . . a . . . come, and share the mystery of the night . . . this peaceful night, suspended forever, enfolded in mist, a sable world flung down before you —a carpet for the queen . . of . . night. (*He turns her toward him.*) For so you are, my beloved . . . I have hunted down the centuries for you, driven by the loneliness of immortality . . . soon, you shall be my bride . . of . . darkness . . . (*He bends toward her throat, his fangs revealed.* WILLY *faints —but before he can reach her,* HELGA *enters from upstairs.*)

HELGA. Count! What means this? (*Indicating his proximity to* WILLY.)

DRACULA. (*Carrying* WILLY, *who has fainted, to the chaise.*) You are the mistress of meanings, fräulein Doctor.

HELGA. (*Crossing* c.) I take it to mean that you have attempted to seduce a dangerously ill woman and she has fainted. Your admiration for your ancestor has led you to a sorry pass, imitating his exploits in this shabby way! (*Crosses* L. U. S. *of desk.*)

DRACULA. (*Crossing to her at* c. *with a grave, sad smile.*) Ah, I fear you misinterpret, learned lady. I beg you to share your knowledge of the mind with me; come, let us talk together, and perhaps you can unlock the secrets of my heart . . . (*Faces out.*)

HELGA. (*Reaching for bell pull but doesn't ring.*) I should call Dr. Seward and have you shown out . . . but—

DRACULA. But you will not? I knew you would not refuse me. (*Then turn and look at each other then*

HELGA *crosses to him.)* Come, let us walk to the end of the terrace, and I will explain myself . . . (*With courtly grace he draws his cape around her shoulders to escort her into the fog and they cross up to the doors.*)

HELGA. (*Pausing in the doorway.*) Count, you must describe to me your early childhood.

DRACULA. (*A pause.*) When I was a boy in Transylvania, I hungered for one thing . . . (*And they exit into the fog. The sinister "Dracula" theme is heard, and* WILLY *begins to move restlessly on the chaise, head rolling back and forth, low moans escaping from her lips.* HARKER *enters from upstairs.*)

HARKER. (*Crossing* c.) Willy? I say, are you quite all right . . . ? (*She is breathing in short, breathy gasps and breaks into a low throaty laugh, holding out a beckoning hand.* HARKER *crosses to her.*) Well, this is flatterin', but do you think we ought . . . (WILLY *pulls him down onto the chaise as she rises off the chaise.*) Oh, never mind . . . (HARKER *slides into the embrace with a will. As he closes his eyes,* WILLY, *becoming more and more erotically deranged, curls up her lip, teeth exposed, and bends toward his throat. There is the howl of a wolf, taken up by an almost bestial scream from* WILLY, *as he breaks from* HARKER *to* c. s. *He stands. Suddenly* WILLY's *eyes clear, she looks at* HARKER *as if seeing him for the first time.*)

WILLY. Jonathan . . . something . . . evil has touched me . . . (*And she faints into his arms.*)

HARKER. Oh, God, not again. (SEWARD *and* VAN HELSING *burst into the room from upstairs.*)

SEWARD. WHAT THE BLOODY HELL ARE YOU UP TO WITH MY NIECE!?

VAN HELSING. (*Crossing* C. *to them.*) Cedric—control yourself!

HARKER. DAMN IT, sir, she's had another fit! Stop attacking me and do something for her! (*He carries her* D. S. *to the chaise placing her on it from the* R. *side —then stands at fireplace.*)

VAN HELSING. (*Kneels at chaise.*) Argue later— Cedric get me some brandy. (SEWARD *crosses to bar, gets glass, places it on* C. *table. He examines her.*) Her pulse is strong, but she is in shock. Where is Helga?

SEWARD. (*Crossing to* R. *of chaise, kneeling next to* WILLY.) Young man, what exactly happened?

HARKER. When I came in, she was, well, rather hysterical, and by the time I could make sense of the situation, she'd fainted. (*As soon as he gets the brandy,* VAN HELSING *begins rubbing it on* WILLY's *wrist.*)

VAN HELSING. I was a fool to leave her. (*He bends to examine* WILLY's *throat more closely and sees the wounds.*) Tssssss . . .

SEWARD. What is it, Abraham?

VAN HELSING. Never mind. But if my diagnosis is correct, we are all in grave danger. (*A wind blows up, and appearing in the doors outlined in the foggy dawn is Godalming, carrying the lifeless, blood-drenched body of* HELGA.)

SEWARD. (*Rising.*) My God . . . !

GODALMING. Someone will pay for this . . . I SWEAR IT!

(*Wolves howl and the lights black out. Moonlight fading last as it silhouettes* GODALMING *and* HELGA *in the doorway.*)

END ACT ONE

ACT TWO

*It is just past sundown, three days later. The weather
has grown even more gloomy and ominous; lower-
ing thunder punctuates the ensuing scene.*

AT RISE: *the study is rather gloomy.* JAMESON *is dusting at the desk. There is a large silver chapel crucifix on the chaise and two boxes with books and
crosses scattered about* D. S. JAMESON *is attempting
to cheer himself in his solitude by singing odd
church hymns and talking to a stuffed owl that
sits on top of the desk.*

JAMESON. (*Takes owl down, blows dust from its
head and places it on the desk.*)
"An' one was a sailor, an' one was a queen,
an' one was a shepherdess on the
    green, (*Thunder clap.*)
they was all of 'em saints of God,
an' I mean, God 'elpin', to be one too . . ."
(*He looks up at the owl. During the speech, he takes
the cross and wrapping paper from the chaise putting
them* U. S. L. *of desk.*) Don't 'ave an opinion, do yer?
. . . shouldn't think so. Well, for my part, it's a dark
time in a narrow place. Poor Miss Willy, as was always merry as a deacon, faintin' and ravin' vile (*Puts
scissors on* C. *table.*) . . . an' Dr. Helga, rest 'er soul,
murdered and under the sod . . . there's none back
from the buryin' yet, an' it's past dark—them high
church folk do go on (*Thunder clap.*) an' here's me own
self (*Puts boxes on floor* U. S. L. *of desk.*) left alone to
mind this whole great pile. Proper bedlam it's be-

comin' around here lately . . . ravin' looney wandering about eatin' anything 'at's helpless, all th' livestock in the county takin' queer, flamin' great bats swoopin', those damn hounds bayin', me with th' bleedin' croup, an' nought for neighbours but that transubstantial Count . . . (*Sits in desk chair.*) nasty piece o' work 'e is. Noble is as noble does, I says. Between the medicals and the peerage the brandy won't last the winter. If Dr. Seward could get anybody else at the pay, I'd be off like a shot . . . but I s'pose I wouldn't 'ave the 'eart to desert 'im, an' besides, who'd believe the references? (*Voices are heard* O. S. JAMESON *to the owl putting it back on top of desk:*) Keep me counsel, there's a good lad . . . (*He starts off* R. *toward the hall. We hear* SEWARD *and* GODALMING *entering in disorder. Sensing the situation,* JAMESON *goes to assist. From the hall we hear:*)

SEWARD. (*Off stage.*) Come along, Gordy, you'll feel better after a nice lie down . . .

JAMESON. (*Exiting.*) Can I 'elp, m' lord?

GODALMING. (*Entering from* R. *followed by* SEWARD *and* JAMESON.) Unhand me, Cedric. (*Crosses* C.) I can make my way alone . . . (*Exerting great effort to stay on his feet.*) . . . I'll have to, now . . . (*He lurches* D. S. *to the desk.*)

SEWARD. (*At stairpost.*) Make coffee, Jameson, and wait till I ring. Is Willy resting?

JAMESON. Yes, sir.

SEWARD. Harker and Van Helsing back yet?

JAMESON. The Professor called to say Mr. Harker would be bringin' 'im back in a motorcar.

SEWARD. From where?

JAMESON. Bad connection, sir, but it sounded like Lands End. Said they'd be in by midevening.

SEWARD. Please stand by, Jameson, it may be a *long* evening.

JAMESON. Right, sir. (*He exits* L.)

SEWARD. (*Stepping* C.) Gordon, old man, would you care for another . . . (*This is superflous*—GODALMING *has been draining the glass of brandy on the desk.*) Oh, . . . hmmm . . . p'rhaps I'll have one m'self. (*Crosses* U. *to bar, empties remaining brandy into snifter.*)

GODALMING. (*Softly.*) Well, she rests in Abraham's bosom now. (*Thunder clap.* GODALMING *crosses* C. *taking glass from* SEWARD.) Looked very peaceful, don't y' think . . . she's at peace, don't y' think, Cedric?

SEWARD. (*Crosses* U.—*gets another full decanter from inside cabinet.*) Dear man, I'm sure of it . . . why didn't you tell me how you two felt about each other? I'd have understood. (*Leaves decanter on top of bar.*)

GODALMING. (*Crosses* D. R. *of chaise.*) She wouldn't hear of it . . . wanted to publish her findings on Renfield before we did anything rash . . . she was lookin' out for my reputation as well. God knows I'd 'ave chucked it all, if she'd only let me. Damndest woman I ever met . . . (JAMESON *enters from* L. *with coffee—crosses to* C. *table and pours.*)

SEWARD. (*Stepping* C.) Just so, just so . . .

GODALMING. . . . damndest woman I ever met . . . (*Sits on* D. S. *end of chaise.*)

JAMESON. Excuse me, sir, but will anyone be dining?

SEWARD. (*A look at* GODALMING.) Neither of us, Jameson, but you could set something for the Professor and Mr. Harker . . . Willy seems to have given up food altogether. (*Taking cup from* JAMESON *and crosses* D. L. *of* C.)

JAMESON. Yes, sir.

GODALMING. Willy's stopped eating?

JAMESON. (*Crossing* D. *to* GODALMING—*give him cup, take snifter.*) This morning at breakfast, m' lord . . . went into a screamin' rage and flung her porridge across the room shoutin' "What's the good of eating—it won't keep you alive once you're dead . . ." (SEWARD *clinks his cup. There is a pause and* JAMESON *says uncomfortably:*) Well, I'd better be about my duties. (*Takes coffee tray and he exits* L.)

SEWARD. . . . That was when we knew she'd taken a turn for the worse.

GODALMING. Shouldn't be botherin' you at all, Cedric, you've got troubles of your own.

SEWARD. (*Crosses to chaise—sits.*) Nonsense—glad of the company. And you shouldn't be by yourself. (*They sit side by side on the chaise.*)

GODALMING. Damned cold of Van Helsing not to attend the funeral, I must say. And I'm surprised at him keepin' company with that Harker, after he went and published that article on Helga . . . smarmy wretch. Can't understand why you're keepin' him 'round for a pet, Seedy.

SEWARD. Because Willy threatened to disown me if I chucked him out. Fact is they seem to have fallen head over heels in love.

GODALMING. Cedric!

SEWARD. I know it's all a bit sudden, but he seems to have done more to perk up her spirits than all of us doctors combined. And I think that's a good value.

GODALMING. Of course it is . . . if you want a journalist in the family.

SEWARD. Gordy . . .

GODALMING. Don't mind me, Cedric I'm just angry and despondent. Christ, if I could just lay hands on whatever killed Helga . . .

SEWARD. Y' know, Gordy, that Dracula fellow was here most of that same evening. Bloody strange blighter 'e was, too.

GODALMING. So I hear.

SEWARD. Have you had anyone check up on him?

GODALMING. The village constable said he'd get 'round to it when he had the time. Gawd, what's the point of havin' a title if no one does what 'y tell 'em to?

SEWARD. Well, I don't trust him, and neither does Van Helsing.

GODALMING. Y' don't say. Well . . . that settles it. He's been too rude to call on me. I'll go call on him . . . have a look at the man's pedigree . . . investigate his blood-lines . . . (*Starts to get up but* SEWARD *sits him back down taking both coffee cups.*)

SEWARD. (*Crosses* L. *to the* U. S. *side of desk, puts down cups.*) Gordon, sit down; you're too drunk to cross the room.

GODALMING. I can still sit a horse! (*Rising.*) I'm going to pay a call on neighbour Dracula! (*Crosses* U. *toward doors.*) Get some answers! (*He turns to leave just as the French doors blow open with a thunder clap and* DRACULA *steps into the room and the doors close.* GODALMING *gives a start.*)

DRACULA. (*Stepping* C.) Good evening, Dr. Seward . . . and this, I take it, must be Lord Godalming. (*Bows to* GODALMING.)

SEWARD. (*At* DRACULA'S L.) Didn't anyone ever teach y' t' knock?

GODALMING. (*At* DRACULA'S R.) So, you're Dracula, eh? I want to ask you some questions about . . .

DRACULA. The late Dr. Van Zandt? Ah, yes. My condolences on the loss of your . . . friend. I fear my absence was noted at the funeral?

GODALMING. We did think it rather queer. We've suffered quite a loss, y' know.

DRACULA. I know more of loss than you can ever comprehend, Lord Godalming. But I see no need to mourn for the dead; in many ways they are to be envied.

GODALMING. What d' y' mean by that? (DRACULA *glances at him.*) Have a little respect, if y' please. (*Crosses* U. *to bar.*)

SEWARD. (*Trying to change the subject.*) I believe you said the other day that you were leaving us soon, Count.

DRACULA. Yes, my affairs here will be concluded this very night. I have come to bid you all farewell.

SEWARD. Yes . . . well . . . goodbye. Nice to have met you. (*He extends a hand which* DRACULA *ignores.*)

DRACULA. (*Crossing* D. R.) I should also like to pay my respects to Miss Murray.

SEWARD. (*Crossing* D. L.) Willy . . . yes . . . well I'm afraid you can't do that. The Professor said no visitors, and she's rather worse today.

DRACULA. Ah, yes . . . the Professor . . . so. I was afraid he'd prove an annoyance.

GODALMING. Now, look here, I've had just about enough of your cryptic remarks . . .

SEWARD. Oh, hush, Gordon!

GODALMING. (*Crossing* D. C.) Don't shush me, Cedric. I want some straight answers to some very simple questions. It's getting so anyone with fancy dress and an accent can claim descent from the Caesars!

DRACULA. (*With deliberate coldness.*) You are a very formidable opponent, Lord Godalming. What is it you wish to know? (*Thunder rumbles.*)

GODALMING. I wish to know about Helga's death for one thing— (*Stepping to* SEWARD.) and about those murders in the village! Seems to me, he started haunting Carfax at just about the right time.

DRACULA. And so suspicion falls on the stranger . . .

GODALMING. You're bloody well right it does. Now I want the truth! (*Rolling up his sleeves, he advances* D. R. *toward* DRACULA.)

DRACULA. (*Face to face with* GODALMING.) The truth. (*Backs him to the chaise. During the following passage* DRACULA *speaks in a low, soft voice, deadly calm, enchanting them with his gaze.*) If I had committed those murders in the village, and destroyed Dr. Van Zandt; (GODALMING *sits.* SEWARD *starts to protest but becomes transfixed and* DRACULA *backs him* D. S. L.) if I were the sinister agent responsible for Miss Murray's condition; if you knew this to be true . . . to whom could you speak, among all humankind, and be believed? (SEWARD *sits on stool.*) Should I reveal to you that I were some creature that sustains itself forever by drinking human blood (*Facing out at* C.) —some vampire out of legend (*A wolf howls in the distance.*) —you would go screaming to a priest, who would tell you . . . such things do not exist. The vampire, in these times, should perish from solitude . . . and disbelief. No, gentlemen; to look upon me and see that truth . . . it is impossible. But enough— I go to claim my own . . . (*He starts* U. S. *for the stairs.* RENFIELD *enters from* L. *interrupting him.*)

RENFIELD. Master! (*Stopping* C. *on first platform.*)

DRACULA. I have subdued them. Speak.

RENFIELD. The Professor and that reporter—they're driving up the east road.

DRACULA. Ah, fate allows me not the tenth part of an hour . . .

RENFIELD. Take her now! Show them your strength, and they shall worship you too!

DRACULA. It cannot be. The spell I make can brook no interruption. I take more than blood tonight . . . I take a bride . . . who weds me in knowledge! (DRACULA *stands gazing up the stairs that lead to* WILLY'S *room.*)

RENFIELD. (*Crossing to* SEWARD.) You'd better be good, Dr. Seward, or I'll have to send you back to your cell. They'd know how to take care of you there. Renfield would tell them how . . . (*And to* GODALMING.) . . . And you, Lord Snot, would you care for a fly? . . . hehehahaha . . . (*He slips a fly from his pouch into* GODALMING'S *mouth.*)

DRACULA. Enough!

RENFIELD. Give them to me . . . why else have you subdued them?

DRACULA. These men amuse me, though they are blind. They ease the tedium of everlasting life . . . but the Professor . . . is another matter. He can see. I have had dreams of this man.

RENFIELD. Dreams, Master?

DRACULA. Long before his time, I dreamt of this encounter. Go! Keep watch! I will have need of you later. (RENFIELD *exits through the French doors. To* SEWARD *and* GODALMING.) Soon your Van Helsing will arrive to tell you what I am—that I am the undead, come from the legends of my people to prey upon your helpless women. But you will refuse to believe such foolishness . . . you will refuse.

RENFIELD. (*At the doors.*) They're coming . . .

DRACULA. Return to your quarters. Tell nothing of what has happened—go! (RENFIELD *exits and* DRACULA *turns back to the others.*) You will remember nothing of my presence . . . nothing has happened . . . nothing was said . . . no visitor has come this night. Good evening, gentlemen . . . (*He exits through the doors. After a moment,* SEWARD *yawns and stretches.* GODALMING *begins to snore.*)

SEWARD. As I was saying, Gordy. GORDY . . . !

GODALMING. What's that? Hmmph! (*He reacts distastefully to a leftover bit of the fly* RENFIELD *fed him.*) Must have . . . nodded off for a moment.

WILLY. (*Appearing at the top of the stairs in agitation.*) I heard voices. Uncle Cedric, who was here just now?

SEWARD. What? Willy, dear, you mustn't leave your bed . . . 'specially at this hour . . .

WILLY. It was Dracula, wasn't it? Didn't he want to see me?

GODALMING. No one's been here, girl, you must have been dreaming.

WILLY. You're lying! You sent him away! Why?

SEWARD. (*Going to her.*) Now, girl, you're overwrought . . . let me help you back to—

WILLY. You've put down one coffin today, will you start on another? I'm stifling in this house—windows bolted shut—no company . . . (*Descending rapidly.*) Why won't you let me *see* him?

SEWARD. You know the Professor gave strict orders—

WILLY. Damn his orders! Damn the lot of you! I'm going to him—NOW! (*She makes a dash for the French doors—*SEWARD *just catches her.*) Let me go!

SEWARD. Gordon! Give me a hand—she's gone hysteric!

GODALMING. (*Leaping to action.*) Steady on, gel, mustn't excite yourself— (WILLY, *with a strength beyond her fraility, cuffs him a smart blow and he falls. She jabs at* SEWARD.)

WILLY. KEEP AWAY FROM ME! I won't be shut in any longer . . . my life's my own . . . I shall do as I please with it!

SEWARD. Dear, no one wants anything but the best for you—

GODALMING. Calmly, gel, steady . . .

WILLY. (*Grabbing the scissors that have been left on the table by the chaise:*) Stop trying to soothe me like a hound! GET . . . BACK . . . (*Brandishing the scissors like a street-fighter, she holds them off, breathing heavily, and makes her way toward the doors as* HARKER *enters to catch her last few lines.*)

HARKER. Willy . . . ! (*She spins around, threatening him with the scissors. Walking slowly toward her, trying to soothe her.*) You playing at high tragedy again . . . modern dress Medea? . . . ritual sacrifice . . . ? Discouragin' habit . . . I had high hopes for you . . . (*He grabs the scissors. She trembles with indecision for a moment, then throws her arms around him.* SEWARD *takes the scissors from* HARKER.) There, there, it's all right . . .

GODALMING. (*Under his breath.*) Good show . . .

VAN HELSING. (*Entering.*) What passes here?

SEWARD. Don't quite know, exactly—it all started . . .

GODALMING. The girl started ravin' caught me one . . .

VAN HELSING. Gentlemen, please, one at a time. (*A pause. They look at each other and begin again.*)

SEWARD. Well, we were dozing off . . .

GODALMING. She seemed to be in a regular fit . . . kept sayin' Dracula'd been here.

VAN HELSING. Dracula? And had he been?

SEWARD. No, that's the strange thing—

WILLY. He was here, I swear it. I heard him!

VAN HELSING. Is all right, Willy. But you have not been alone with him.

WILLY. No! (VAN HELSING *examines her throat.*)

Van Helsing. The evidence is to the contrary. You tell me untruth, Willy.

Seward. What's this, Abraham?

Willy. But I'm not lying—why are you badgering me?

Harker. Is this really necessary, Professor?

Van Helsing. You know it is! Willy, the cross I give you to wear—why do you take it off?

Willy. But I didn't . . . it was there . . . I don't know how it— Oh why won't you leave me alone . . . !

Van Helsing. Because I must have truth. Dracula was by you—if not this evening, then last night . . .

Willy. No! I swear . . . please . . .

Seward. Abraham!

Van Helsing. Never mind, Willy, is enough . . . I am foolish to accuse you . . . forgive me? Help her to her room, Jonathan.

Harker. (*Crossing down to her.*) Come along, then . . . back to durance vile. (Willy *takes* Harker's *outstretched hand, and they head for the stairs.*) We can sit on the edge of your bed and say things the old folks shouldn't hear.

Willy. (*Pausing at the foot of the stairs.*) Adieu everyone. Don't worry, I'm quite all right, I . . . good night. (*She precedes* Harker *up the stairs.* Van Helsing *rings for* Jameson *and goes to pour himself a brandy.*)

Van Helsing. Is remarkable . . .

Seward. Abraham Van Helsing, what are you playing at?

Van Helsing. Playing! I am playing nothing! I'm trying to understand.

Jameson. (*Entering.*) Did you ring for me, Dr. Seward?

Van Helsing. I did, Jameson. Go up to the sanitorium and fetch down this patient, Renfield. Be careful he does not escape you. Is all right, Cedric?

SEWARD. Yes, I suppose. Off you go, Jameson. (JAMESON *exits*.) Why do you want Renfield, Abraham?

VAN HELSING. Because he escapes so often. Never mind, you shall see, Cedric. Let me begin at the beginning: This morning I talked to the port master at Tate Hill Pier.

SEWARD. Then that's where you and Harker have been all day?

VAN HELSING. There, and other places. Listen. He told me that six weeks ago the ship, *Demeter,* ran aground off Land's End, just after sundown. There was no sign of life on board, except for a huge bat which flew instantly from the rigging. And there was no cargo on board, except for a single coffin-like box which contained a few ounces of dried earth.

SEWARD. Where is this all leading us, Abraham?

VAN HELSING. To the truth, I hope. This box, which had been impounded as evidence, vanished mysteriously later this same night. (HARKER *enters*.)

SEWARD. What does this have to do with Willy?

VAN HELSING. (*Over excited.*) He had to have the box! His coffin, filled with his native soil; exactly as the legend says!

GODALMING. Hmmm . . . Cedric, do you know what the devil he's talkin' about?

HARKER. I do. At least I do since this morning.

GODALMING. I didn't ask you! Damn scandalmonger! How dare you publish that . . .

VAN HELSING. Gordon, please, this is not the time.

HARKER. I'm sorry if my article upset you, Lord Godalming, but for right now you must hear the Professor out. I know it's hard to grasp, but . . . (JAMEson *has entered with* RENFIELD *in tow.* RENFIELD *is wearing a straight jacket.*)

RENFIELD. No, it's not! It's easy, the simplest thing in the world, if you've half a mind; but there's not a worthwhile brain in this entire room except mine . . . and his. (*He gestures to* VAN HELSING.) You can grasp it, can't you; yes . . . I can tell.

VAN HELSING. Yes, I think so, Mr. Renfield. I am Dr. Van . . . What is this . . . (*Indicating the straight jacket.*) . . . release this man. (JAMESON *starts to protest.*) Do as I say! I don't know how a thing like this could have happened. You sit right here in the seat of honor. (*He indicates the chair by the desk.* RENFIELD *sits in the chair and* VAN HELSING *sits near him on a stool.*) Now, tell me this theory of yours.

GODALMING and SEWARD. (*Groaning.*) Oh no . . . Professor, must you really . . .

VAN HELSING. SILENCE! (*Addressing* RENFIELD *again:*) Don't listen to them. You just talk to me, yes?

RENFIELD. It's life, you see; the great secret of eternal life. Now contemplate the ancients: Adam; Abraham; Methuselah. What is our span of years compared to theirs . . . nothing. Well, what was it, what was their secret? I'll tell you! THEY KNEW THAT TO PROLONG LIFE, YOU HAD TO AB-SORB LIFE! LIVING, BREATHING FLESH, STILL PULSATING WITH THE LIVING BLOOD. We're out of practice these days . . . but slowly, bit by bit, I'm rediscovering the entire process. Starting small, of course.

VAN HELSING. Who taught you all this, Mr. Renfield?

RENFIELD. No one. I made it up. 'Tis extempore from my mother wit.

VAN HELSING. (*Laughs.*) That's very good. Come

now, Mr. Renfield. I should like very much to meet your teacher. He must be a very great man.

RENFIELD. You'd like to meet him? Perhaps I could . . . I, I think maybe I could arrange to— (*Thunder and lightening.*) NO, NO! It's forbidden! He made me swear. I see! You're trying to trick me. No, no. No more words, no more . . . (*He is in great agitation, shaking his head, mumbling: "No, no more, no . . ."*)

VAN HELSING. Just one more. Your teacher, was he not Count Dracula?

RENFIELD. No! You mustn't speak that name— never. He'll think I've betrayed him. Tell him it wasn't me that said his name . . . promise . . . ?

VAN HELSING. I promise Mr. Renfield, as soon as I meet him again, I'll tell him it wasn't you. (*He puts his hand on* RENFIELD's *shoulder.*) You can go back to your room now, but I'd like to hear the rest of your theory later.

RENFIELD. Yes, I'd like that.

JAMESON. (*Starting to lead him off.*) Be a good boy, now. Come along.

RENFIELD. Did you hear how he understood me? I'm not mad, you know, just ahead of my time . . . (*JAMESON pulls him off.*)

VAN HELSING. How long has he been like that?

SEWARD. Y' mean his fly eatin' business? That all started about a month ago.

HARKER. Professor—is there a connection do you think?

VAN HELSING. Yes. I am sure of it.

SEWARD. All right, Abraham, explain yourself. What's wrong with Willy? Why all these questions? What does the shipwreck have to do with it?

GODALMING. And Dracula, don't forget him . . .

HARKER. Professor, you must make it clear to them.

VAN HELSING. (*Taking a deep breath and looking at them pointedly.*) Cedric, Wilhelmina is the prey of a vampire. Her blood is being drawn from her veins nightly—through those two wounds in her neck . . . though as yet I think she knows not herself what happens.

GODALMING. Tommyrot!

SEWARD. But you can't expect us to accept this—vampires are myths, like banshees.

VAN HELSING. From you, Cedric? I had expected a more open mind.

GODALMING. Vampires. . . .

HARKER. But you must believe. The Professor has shown me that . . .

GODALMING. There is nothing in England, sir, that behaves like that!

VAN HELSING. They said that, no doubt, when the plague struck London. Yes, my friends, the vampire arrived on the *Demeter*, and walks among us.

HARKER. It's Dracula—don't you see? He's the village murderer—he is the Whitby Terror.

SEWARD. It's just not possible! I can't believe what I'm hearing!

VAN HELSING. Aeah! Your minds are closed to me! John! Did you ever finish developing photo you took?

HARKER. Yes, it's still upstairs, but it's the strangest thing . . .

VAN HELSING. Never mind, just fetch it, please.

HARKER. All right. If you think it will help. (*He exits.*)

GODALMING. Really, Abraham, this is absurd!

VAN HELSING. Gordon, yesterday I go to Oxford University, consult Almanach Gotha. Family of Dracula extinct for four hundred years!

Seward. I won't listen!

Van Helsing. You *must* listen! In his perfect arrogance he tell us everything he is, remember? He describe the vampire perfectly, and when he speak of Vlad Dracula, he speaks of himself.

Seward. Rubbish!

Van Helsing. I believe his legend—is too dangerous not to! He can send his spirit into the animals. He commands the elements, the rain, the lightning. He lives by drinking human blood, and he can bend minds to his will.

Seward. Bends minds . . . drinks blood . . . sleeps in a box . . .

Van Helsing. In his coffin!

Seward. Abraham!

Van Helsing. Yes! He must return to it by dawn or be destroyed by the rays of the sun. Mr. Harker and I search all day for this coffin.

Godalming. You went through Carfax Abbey?

Van Helsing. Yes, but if coffin was there, he have moved it. Carfax is—what do you call it? —red herring.

Seward. I've heard enough, Abraham. For God's sake, this is supposed to be the twentieth century. Listen—I've got a very sick girl on my hands and no physical remedy. If you want to continue this damn theorizin', publish an article in the Lancet! At the moment I need somethin' practical t' do!

Harker. (*Entering.*) Professor, here's the photo . . .

Van Helsing. Never mind, Jonathan. (*Crossing to* Cedric.) For the moment is practical to watch her hourly for any change—stay by her day and night, and be prepared to make transfusion, if necessary. If you know not your blood types, Cedric, take samples and test, yes?

SEWARD. That's sound medical advice. Gordy, can I impose on you?

GODALMING. Certainly. Glad to do it. Lead on, Cedric. (*They exit upstairs.*)

VAN HELSING. No one believed Galileo, either . . .

HARKER. How could they be so blind. Damn, I was afraid of this.

VAN HELSING. You are very perceptive young man. Gordon read your article in paper this afternoon. Did you not promise me not to publish?

HARKER. Hated to do that, but if I hadn't fed 'em something, they'd have sent a real muckraker up here. Well, news is news! And it is a damned odd business.

VAN HELSING. Yes, perhaps damnder odder than you think. That photograph you develop of Dracula—you (*Takes photo from* HARKER.) have picture of baronial fireplace, but no Count standing in front, is correct? Is correct!

HARKER. Yes, and it's impossible—I've been using that Grafflex for years, and haven't missed yet.

VAN HELSING. You did not miss. Grafflex is use silver nitrate plate, yes? With cross-hair finder lens, yes?

HARKER. Yes . . .

VAN HELSING. And what you photograph will never appear in silver, framed on a cross!

HARKER. But this is proof. Why didn't you tell the others?

VAN HELSING. They would take it as proof only that you are incompetent photographer. It is as if something had closed their minds. And there is more.

HARKER. Sir?

VAN HELSING. The victim of the vampire does not always die the long death. They may rise again to feed on the living—they themselves may become vampires.

HARKER. You mean if Willy . . .

VAN HELSING. No, no. There I fear something more complex. The girls in the village, poor Helga, killed on the instant and drained of blood. But Willy . . . she has been failing for weeks, yet still she lives, still she is in the netherworld. I think this is some hideous ritual, too horrible for her to remember. He has some special purpose.

HARKER. My God—something must be done now—

VAN HELSING. Yes—we must expose him. We must convince Cedric and Lord Godalming his very existence before we can hope to destroy him!

HARKER. How? You've done everything but an illustrated lecture on vampires.

VAN HELSING. But if they were to see someone they already knew—someone who had become undead . . .

HARKER. Helga!

VAN HELSING. Just so. If she be vampire, she shall rise . . .

HARKER. Lord, how horrible!

VAN HELSING. But if we seal her tomb with holy cross, she cannot escape to kill . . . and she remain to serve as proof! Come, hurry, there is not much time!

HARKER. All right. I'm with you. But what about Willy? We can't leave her unguarded?

VAN HELSING. Nor shall we. (*Rings bell pull.*) We will set the good Mr. Jameson to watch—while we visit Helga's crypt.

HARKER. I'll get the car.

VAN HELSING. No, let us walk. No need to alarm Gordon until we have certain proof. (JAMESON *enters.*) Ah, Jameson, Mr. Harker and I must go out for a while. I want you to take this cross and sit here on the steps. *Do not let go the cross.* Understand?

JAMESON. No, sir.

VAN HELSING. Will you do as I ask?

JAMESON. Yes, sir!

VAN HELSING. Good! We shall return as soon as may be. You, too, John, take cross and hold fast.

HARKER. I'd rather a revolver—but I'll do as you say, Professor. Are you sure Willy's safe?

VAN HELSING. No—but she will surely perish if we cannot make the danger understood. You have much fondness for Willy, not so?

HARKER. Need you ask?

VAN HELSING. Good! We are allies to the end of this, yes?

HARKER. Done!

VAN HELSING. Come! (*They exit, leaving* JAMESON *on the steps.*)

JAMESON. (*Looking at the cross.*) An' me a Calvinist . . . oh, well, if it makes their 'eart rest easier, I s'pose there's no 'arm. If me old Mum could see me now . . . (*There is a black out.*) 'Ere NOW! What th'— (*The lights are restored.* JAMESON *is standing with his sweater over his head, and* RENFIELD *has the cross, laughing.*) Oh, crikey . . . Renfield, you blinkin' looney, come back 'ere wi' that! (*He chases* REN-FIELD *out.*)

(*After a moment* GODALMING *enters from the stairs and goes to the phone by the desk.*)

GODALMING. Godalming here, Alice—put me through to the manor house. Jenkins, are you there? Yes, tell Lady Doris I'll be spending the night at Seward's—weather's too beastly to ride.

(*There is an amazing lightning and thunderclap, and
the lights go out.*)

GODALMING. Good God! No, Jenkins, not you. Something's just gone awry with the lights here. Any rate,
I . . . (*A reverb voiceover of* HELGA *is heard whispering:* "*Gor . . . don . . .*") My God! . . . No,
Jenkins, not you . . . I thought I heard . . . (*Voiceover: Gor . . . don . . .*) . . . Goodby, Jenkins.
(*Shaken, he hangs up the phone.*) Who . . . who's
callin' me? (*There is another terrific thunderclap, and*
GODALMING *jumps up. He is trembling, tries to pour
himself another drink.*) . . . get a grip, now . . .
strain's beginnin' t' tell. (*Crosses to the fireplace.*)
Here's to the Professor's creature . . . (HELGA *appears at the French doors behind him. Her hair is down
and her burial gown is blowing in the misty wind.*
GODALMING *senses she is there and wheels around and
gasps.*)

HELGA. (*Voice over.*) I am cold, Gordon . . . so
cold. Let me in . . . warm me . . .

GODALMING. No! Stay away! I buried you . . .

HELGA. (*Voice over.*) Gordon, my love, there is a
way for us to be united forever. . . .

GODALMING. What . . . ? (*He begins to cross slowly
to the doors.*)

HELGA. (*Voice over.*) You thought I had deserted
you, did you not? No . . . I have studied with the
Master, learned the secret that will make you mine
forever . . .

GODALMING. (*He opens his arms to her.*) Helga . . .

(*The doors swing open and she enters.*)

HELGA. . . . the Übermensch gave me the kiss of life, mastery over the peasants and churchmongers for all time . . . I will bind you to me in immortality, Gordon, my darling, and together we shall bring Walpurgisnacht down upon the world . . . (*She is laughing maniacally.* GODALMING *slips to his knees, turning to look up at her.*)

GODALMING. Helga, you are mad . . .

HELGA. Mad or no, I am your mistress . . . (*As she is laying him on the floor:*) Come . . . submit . . . soon . . . you will understand . . . (*Fangs revealed, she kneels by his side and bends toward his throat. There is a flash of lightning and thunder, and* DRACULA —*swooping in through the mist*—*grabs her by the throat. Gasping.*) Meister . . .

DRACULA. You importunate glutton! You think in your lust to defy my will? You shall have what I choose to give, when I choose to give it! His blood is not yours to take! (*He releases his strangle hold on her, flinging her to the chaise.*) Rise, Lord Godalming. (GODALMING *stands.*) You will, forget, for now, your degrading passion for this would-be valkyrie, and learn true submission. You will forget what has passed . . . you will bear yourself with the nobility to which you aspire. (*To* HELGA.) Take him into the night, fondle him, do what you are accustomed to do, but for now his life must be preserved. He is my slave before he becomes your plaything. GO! (*Gazing after them as they exit.*) The English public school system will never cease to amaze me . . . (*He crosses* D. S. *to listen to the baying of the hounds.*) Ah, the children of the night, what music they make . . . sing . . . sing to your lord who has come to claim his bride . . . cry praise to a heart fulfilled that has lain fallow these many centuries. (*In a hoarse, conjuring whis-*

per.) Wilhelmina . . . come to me . . . come, as I bid you . . . (WILLY *appears at the head of the stairs, in a negligee, her gaze vacant; she is responding to* DRACULA's *call, unaware of the impulse drawing her down the stairs. She glides into the room and gradually becomes aware of* DRACULA's *presence.*)

WILLY. Count Dracula.

DRACULA. You know me now?

WILLY. Yes.

DRACULA. And you fear me not? . . . you join me freely?

WILLY. Yes.

DRACULA. (*He crosses* U. S. *and holds out a beckoning hand.*) Come . . . rest . . . (WILLY *moves into his arms. There is a pause—they kiss. He leads her to the chaise, she lies down.*) Rest, and listen to my voice . . . you are soon to recover your strength . . . my power shall restore you to everlasting beauty . . . (*Slowly* DRACULA's *hand reaches out to touch* WILLY's *throat, caress it ever so slightly, and withdraw. He stands over her immobile for a terrible moment, then wheels* U. S. *and turns, raising his arms over her in invocation:*)

Now by my powers of most dread black,
By bonds of blood your soul shall cleave to mine.
My covenant seals you wife to my desire,
Mistress eternal of the vaults of Night,
Until the Sun shall die
Dracula, Lord of Darkness calls you,
Dracula, whom no mortal may deny.

(*On concluding his chant, Dracula swoops* D. S. *and takes her body in his arms, turning to face the audience. He lowers her to the ground.*) Now you are mine forever, your soul mingled with mine, your body made immortal, your veins filled with the power . . . of my blood . . . (*Tearing open his shirt with his* D. S. *hand, removing his brooch, he rips it across his chest tearing open a vein.*) Drink . . . my beloved, and be my bride till time has stopped.

(WILLY *places her lips to his chest and drinks. Then he embraces her feverishly—she responds with deranged ardor. Flashing his fangs, he kisses her, and is just drawing back to sink his teeth in her throat when suddenly a beam of light appears through the French doors. It is* HARKER *and* VAN HELSING. HARKER *is wearing his cross.* VAN HELSING *is carrying a large cross.* DRACULA *reacts violently in fear and anger and releases* WILLY. *She sinks to her knees.*)

HARKER. Willy!

VAN HELSING. Stay by Willy—guard her! (VAN HELSING *holds* DRACULA *at bay with the cross as* HARKER *goes to* WILLY *and holds her. She is struggling violently, growling, trying to reach* DRACULA.)

DRACULA. She is mine now, in spite of your meddling! She is my bride forever, sealed with my blood.

VAN HELSING. You lie! She is sealed with the blood of Christ! So long as there is life in her body she is not wholly your creature. John, take her upstairs—now!

HARKER. What about you?

VAN HELSING. Go! fetch Cedric! Hurry! I shall endeavor to entertain Count Dracula. (HARKER *rushes upstairs with* WILLY *during the previous speech.* DRACULA *rushes the stairs, but* VAN HELSING *holds the cross in front of him, pushing* DRACULA *back with it. It burns him, and* DRACULA *is forced back across the room.*)

Dracula. You are very learned, Van Helsing.

Van Helsing. And you, Voivoide Dracula, Vlad the necromancer . . .

Dracula. You know me.

Van Helsing. I think I have studied all my life to know you.

Dracula. Strange, that a man who hungers for knowledge would oppose my will . . . come to me, Van Helsing, and I will give you to know the meaning of eternity . . . (*He extends his hand.*)

Van Helsing. We are opposed for eternity! You devour men, body and soul.

Dracula. You have lived long, Van Helsing. You have seen war, disease, famine . . . you have watched men grow old, decay, and die, with one thought in their minds: Why? But if I take Wilhelmina now . . . if I choose to make her immortal . . . as you love her, you cannot deny her my gift. Come with us, Van Helsing—together we shall ride the dark winds past the edge of time.

Van Helsing. It can never be. I serve Heaven, and can never learn to reign in Hell. (*He raises cross.*)

Dracula. Is your faith so very strong? Submit, Van Helsing. My legions grow nightly. (*He gestures and crosses* d. s. Helga, Godalming *and* Renfield *enter.*)

Van Helsing. To save her I would gladly perish: To save the world from your evil I shall be the instrument of your destruction.

Helga. Join us, Professor . . . we have need of your wisdom . . .

Renfield. (*Darting forward from the French doors, he snatches the cross.*) The Master commands you, you must obey . . .

Godalming. Come along old fellow . . . (*Unarmed

and surrounded, VAN HELSING *backs* D. *around the chaise to the fireplace.*)

VAN HELSING. Gordon! Not you too!

DRACULA. No, Professor, he still lives on your side of the great abyss . . . but tonight I shall have you all.

(*During all this,* HELGA, RENFIELD, *and perhaps even* GODALMING *have kept up whispered, seductive commands to* VAN HELSING *to join them.* DRACULA, *ready for the kill.*)

DRACULA. NOW YOU SHALL BE MINE! (*He leaps up on the chaise, but* VAN HELSING *grabs the fireplace implements. Forming them into a cross he holds* DRACULA *back as* SEWARD, HARKER *and* JAMESON *enter* —SEWARD *firing a pistol.*)

HARKER. Professor! (HARKER *leaps the banister and knocks out* RENFIELD.)

JAMESON. Jesus, Billy be damned! (*He rushes* HELGA, *holding out the cross from around his neck to protect him.*)

SEWARD. Good Lord, Helga! (SEWARD *bashes* GODALMING *saying:*) Sorry old man! (HELGA *breaks from* JAMESON *whom she has been trying to strangle, and attempts to stop* SEWARD, *but* HARKER *grabs her and holds her.*)

DRACULA. ENOUGH! You have won this round, Van Helsing, but our little game is not yet ended!

VAN HELSING. Your strength lies in others' disbelief —I believe . . . many things.

DRACULA. Yours is the wisdom of a petty lifetime, mine is the work of centuries. (*He crosses up to the French doors.*) I shall return to claim my bride . . . and when I do, not one of you shall 'scape my wrath. . . . (*Having backed out onto the terrace, he flings up both arms and a tremendous wind fills the stage. There is a blackout, a strobe, an explosion;* Dracula *disappears and a glowing, giant bat swoops from the stage out over the audience.)*

END ACT TWO

ACT THREE

*Roughly a half hour later—state of total seige.
Godalming is prone on the floor with a pillow and
blanket; Willy is on the couch receiving a transfusion from Harker. Van Helsing is at the desk
reading while Seward supervises the transfusion.
Jameson enters.*

Van Helsing. Is Helga secured?

Jameson. Yes, sir. We locked her upstairs and put a
cross through the latch.

Van Helsing. Good! Go to the root celler and bring
me all the sprouted garlic you can find, then get all
the surveyor's stakes from where they are digging the
new wing. Quickly man! There is not time to lose!

*(Jameson exits. Godalming sits up, staring dazedly at
mid-air, snatches at something, and eats it.)*

Godalming. The blood is the wife . . . (Seward,
having seen this, reaches over and slaps Godalming
smartly.) Ahhh! I say, what's happened?

Seward. Well, there was a bit of a ruckus and you
had to be conked.

Godalming. I feel dreadful.

Seward. You just ate a fly.

(Godalming rushes upstairs to be sick.)

Van Helsing. Poor man.

Seward. Hmph—never thought it would come to
this—worse than the Sepoy massacre of '57. I say,

Abraham, I must have been mad not to believe you but I'm still terribly confused . . . (*He has crossed to* Willy *and is removing the needle from her arm.*) Obviously we're in a bad way, what with Dracula bein' such a rotter and all . . .

Van Helsing. Now that he is discovered, he will destroy us all if he can. Thank God now you and Gordon believe.

Harker. (*The needle having been removed from his arm.*) Doctor, has it worked?

Seward. I hope so, John. She will be stronger at least.

Van Helsing. But so long as Dracula lives, she is in his power.

Harker. (*Rising from his chair.*) Oh God! (Seward *and* Van Helsing *move to support* Harker *and sit him back down.*)

Van Helsing. There my boy, now stretch out, or you'll feel quite sick.

Harker. What's to be done, Professor? Is Willy incurable?

Van Helsing. It will be hard to tell until she wakes. She has been infected with Dracula's blood. Perhaps transfusion from you will prove the counterspell.

(Godalming *pokes his head in at this moment, and hears the next two lines . . . after which he cogitates at the head of the stairs.*)

Seward. What if we try the same medicine on poor Helga?

Van Helsing. She is undead. For poor Helga there is only one cure . . . a stake driven through the heart.

Seward. Lord. Don't tell Godalming . . . not yet anyway.

JAMESON. (*Entering with a bundle of stakes and bulbs of garlic.*) Here are the things you wanted, Professor. I know you're busy, but what's the garlic for?

VAN HELSING. For keeping bats away. I want you to put some over every door and window in the house. Begin in the hall.

(JAMESON *exits with the garlic.* GODALMING *re-enters.*)

SEWARD. Here, old man, let me get you a drink.

GODALMING. (*On the stairs.*) Where's Helga?

VAN HELSING. We've locked her in her room, Gordon.

GODALMING. There's no hope then?

VAN HELSING. I'm afraid not.

SEWARD. Gordon, old man.

GODALMING. (*Coming* D. *the stairs.*) There'll be war with Germany, you know. Two years, three years, but it will come. I did everything I could, risked my reputation, and it's no good. They won't listen, neither side will listen. I shan't sit in the House next term, I'm afraid . . . (*With an anguished cry he breaks* U. S.) Helga! . . . my Rhinemaiden . . . my maimed darling . . . Seward, I'm going out on the terrace to get some air.

VAN HELSING. Gordon . . .

HARKER. Wait. (HARKER *hands* GODALMING *a wooden cross. There is a pause of reconciliation, and* GODALMING *exits through the French doors.*)

SEWARD. Poor chappie.

VAN HELSING. You know what must be done . . .

SEWARD. Yes, I suppose you're right, but we'll have to wait 'till Godalming's well away.

VAN HELSING. She is safe enough for the present, I

suppose. Cedric, put that equipment away. And would you see how Jameson is progressing with the garlic? I want every access covered—I'm going to look for Renfield.

SEWARD. Right. (SEWARD *exits* U. *the stairs.* VAN HELSING *crosses to* WILLY.)

VAN HELSING. John, Willy may come 'round shortly. Keep your cross by you, and on no account become . . . intimate with her. You have given enough blood to this cause already. For the present, as you love her, shun her.

HARKER. Very well, Professor. (*In a low deadly whisper as he picks up one of the stakes:*) God I want a fair chance at that monster.

VAN HELSING. We shall have it, never fear. I trust his arrogance as well as his lust. Hold steadfast, as you British are so famous for doing. Patience will have it in the end.

HARKER. By Heaven, I hope you're right.

VAN HELSING. Trust me, for her sake; it's the only way. (VAN HELSING *exits.* JAMESON *enters from* S. R. *with garlic and exits* S. L. HARKER *looks* D. *at the sleeping* WILLY, *then goes to the side board for a brandy. Brandy in hand he crosses* D. R. *below the fireplace and sits.* WILLY *is coming to—she gasps.* HARKER *jumps* U., *startled, and remembering what the Professor said, thrusts his cross toward her. Embarrassed at his own fear, he lowers the cross.*)

HARKER. I—I'm sorry, the Professor said to . . .

WILLY. Yes . . . it's all right . . . I remember. I remember. Oh God, I remember! Oh, Jonathan, what must I seem to you. If you ever loved me, you would do well to leave me, and remember me fondly, as the song goes.

HARKER. Willy . . . (*She turns to look at him.*) You mustn't give up hope.

WILLY. Jonathan . . . (HARKER *goes to touch her, thinks better of it and withdraws his hand.* WILLY *grabs his wrist.*) It's alright to touch me. The mood isn't on me right now. (HARKER *rushes into her arms. They hold each other tightly, sitting on the chaise.*) Did I have a transfusion?

(GODALMING *enters unseen from the French doors, watches them for a moment, leaves his cross on the side board and exits upstairs.*)

HARKER. Yes.

WILLY. It was you, wasn't it? I was dimly aware. It felt like being carried from Hieronymous Bosch into William Blake and the first sunny day at Brighton. I don't know how I should be getting through this if you hadn't come snooping with your camera. (*He kisses her fondly on the nose.*) Help me up, will you?

HARKER. Are you sure you're strong enough?

WILLY. No. And I never will be unless I get some food. I haven't eaten since yesterday. Help me to the pantry, if you please.

HARKER. (*Rising.*) Don't be silly. I'll gladly fetch you something.

WILLY. Oh, no! It's getting so the very sight of this chaise is enough to ruin my appetite.

HARKER. All right. (*Helping her up, he leads her around the chaise* U. S. C.) Steady on. There's a bit of literature *I've* been meaning to discuss with *you*. It goes on in a dreary monotone for a while, mentions something about richer and poorer . . . odds and ends like that. Must talk you into doing the thing one of these days. (*She looks up at him realizing what he is saying with joy, and at the same time fear of what she may be-*

come. *She starts to protest.*) No. You needn't give me an answer now. I think we should wait 'till we've known each other at least a week. (*He smiles, she laughs, and they embrace. He has put up a good front.*) Well, on to the pantry. And don't stray out of my sight—I don't trust you literary types with the silver . . .

(*They exit* L. *A moment later* GODALMING *enters from the stairs with* HELGA *in tow.*)

HELGA. Ah, my good Gordy, you have rescued me! Now I shall give to you the kiss of life, and we shall be united for all time . . .

GODALMING. Yes, my love, we shall have eternity to ourselves . . . free from interruptions . . . free from duty . . . free from those who would have profaned your beauty with a stake . . . free to live . . . (*He crosses* D. L. *to the desk, realizing what he must do.*)

HELGA. Yes, Gordon. They will never have power over us again . . . the Master has promised. (*She crossses* D. *from the platform.* GODALMING *moves in front of the desk chair, hiding the stake that* HARKER *has left there.*) Now I will rescue you . . . from mortality . . . from this troublesome existence . . . from those who would make your life an endless sacrifice. Now you shall be my consort and be served by kings. Parliament and all England shall grovel at our feet! Join me, liebchen . . . (*She takes his hand, without looking at him, and begins to lead him to the terrace.* GODALMING *picks up the stake, unseen by* HELGA, *and holds it behind him.*) . . . in eternity . . .

(*They exit. There is a pause, then a bloodcurdling scream, echoed by a lone wolf.* GODALMING *reenters with blood-stained hands and pauses in the doorway.*)

GODALMING. Ah, my darling . . . you could have had me . . . but you shall never have England. (*He crosses to the desk and gets a revolver.* SEWARD *and* VAN HELSING *rush on, drawn by* HELGA's *scream.*)

SEWARD. What was that?

GODALMING. I have set Helga free, gentlemen. Believe me, there is no cause for alarm. (*He is crossing to the French doors.*)

VAN HELSING. Gordon! No! We need you!

GODALMING. (*Crossing to the French doors.*) I'm past any use, I'm afraid. Don't try to follow, please. I must make a great reckoning, as Marlowe said, in a little room . . . (*He exits to the terrace. A pause, and we hear the shot.*)

SEWARD. Bravest man I've ever known.

HARKER. (*Rushes on from the pantry.*) Professor . . . what was that shot? (SEWARD *simply points to the terrace.* HARKER *turns to look out the French doors.*) Oh, my Lord . . .

WILLY. (*Rushes on.*) What on earth . . . ?

SEWARD. Willy, no . . . (*Seeing the two bodies* WILLY *recoils and crosses* D. *to the desk and sits.* JAMESON *runs on.*)

JAMESON. Sir, has something happened? I heard a shot.

SEWARD. On the terrace, Jameson . . . there's been a terrible accident. . . .

HARKER. Godalming did what had to be done; now he's done for himself, I'm afraid.

JAMESON. What's to be done with the bodies, sir?

VAN HELSING. (*Slowly becoming manic.*) You may as well leave them. There will be others before morning.

SEWARD. Abraham! (HARKER *moves to* WILLY *and puts his hands on her shoulders.*)

Van Helsing. Cedric, can you tell me please, the day?

Seward. Saturday, Professor, but why?

Van Helsing. "It was upon a Saturday, they came to take the Lord away" . . . (*There is a pause. Then suddenly* Van Helsing *begins to laugh bitterly, with rising hysteria. He sits* D. R.)

Seward. Abe, get a grip, old man—no laughin' matter here, y' know— (*The laughter continues.*) Come now, steady on, don't give way . . . (Van Helsing *takes a small vial from his pocket and scoops up some suspicious-looking powder with his thumbnail and snorts a healthy couple of nostrilsful. He replaces the vial.*)

Van Helsing. Ah, my dear friends, forgive me. It is unseemly, perhaps, this outburst. Everyone's life imperilled, blood ritual in a Christian home, and at such a moment the divine irrational intervene . . . even at such a moment King Laugh come and whisper in my ear, "Here I am!" Oh, my friends, it is a strange world, a sad world, full of miseries and woes and troubles, but when King Laugh come, he make them all dance the tune he plays. Believe me, my friends, he is good to come, and kind. And I do not think I shall laugh again this long while . . . but enough.

Seward. Jonathan, will you give us a hand? For now, we'll put them in the servant's kitchen. Sorry, Jameson, but you can take your meals in the pantry for the duration.

Jameson. Understood, sir.

Seward. Abraham, you'd best keep Willy company.

Van Helsing. Of course. (Seward, Harker *and* Jameson *exit to the terrace.* Willy *rises and crosses slowly to* Van Helsing.) How is it with you, Willy?

WILLY. It comes and goes. Are you so certain I'll not try to sink my teeth in you?

VAN HELSING. Nothing in this life is certain. The scripture says perfect love casteth out fear . . .

WILLY. (*Moves in on him and bends over him, then kisses him on the head and sinks to her knees, embracing him.*) Oh, Uncle Tulip, forgive me . . . my nerves are raw . . . this whole thing is so ghastly . . . never knowing when you'll turn on those dearest to you. Tell me . . .

VAN HELSING. My dear?

WILLY. Do you think I will survive?

VAN HELSING. Do you remember as a child, when you were so ill, and we were all so worried? The night your fever broke, you waked and said that a lady with a star had come to visit you. (*Noticing the ring on her right hand:*) This ring, it was your Mother's, you know. This time too, the light will come. We will release you from his evil, I swear it. Until then you must hover between light and darkness . . . it cannot be easy, and you have been very brave.

WILLY. Uncle Tulip?

VAN HELSING. Hmmm?

WILLY. Does God speak Dutch?

VAN HELSING. (*Smiling.*) Sometimes, you precocious vixen, he even speaks broken English. Now, you be brave for Jonathan, and I'll put up a good front for Cedric and Jameson, and it should even out.

WILLY. (*Rising, holding his hands.*) You are deliberately naive, and socially devious . . . and I love you, very much.

VAN HELSING. And I you . . . (*They embrace. SEWARD, HARKER and JAMESON enter somewhat grimly.*)

SEWARD. She looked like a child . . . . Abraham, we

are goin' to have to cobble up some convincin' death
certificates.

HARKER. And notify the Prime Minister and Lady
Doris—grim business.

VAN HELSING. Mister Jameson, do you think you
could find us some coffee? It's going to be a long night.

JAMESON. I'll have some up in a trice, sir. Would
some sandwiches help?

HARKER. The very thing. (JAMESON *exits*.) Professor,
what's our plan?

VAN HELSING. We must play the cards we are dealt.
We have only foiled him temporarily. He performs in
ritual fashion—therefore we must try to discover the
counter-spell. We know he must return for Willy . . .

HARKER. Over my dead body—

VAN HELSING. Don't tempt circumstance . . . at
night he is all-powerful, but he must sleep in his
coffin by day.

HARKER. If only we could find that bloody coffin and
destroy it . . . leave him to the mercy of the sun.

SEWARD. We don't even know where to begin.

HARKER. It must be somewhere.

VAN HELSING. Yes, somewhere, then somewhere else.
Always, we keep searching, coming so close . . . ah
. . . he traps me in my own knowledge!

HARKER. What, sir?

SEWARD. How's this?

VAN HELSING. He see I know of his coffin, and so he
move it. It is a ploy—what do you call it? —a gambit.
No! We go no more into his field—when his lust drive
him here, I shall have him! I play no more his game—
he shall play mine . . . to the finish.

WILLY. If you must kill him, strike with no malice
in your hearts. He was very noble once, and he is
so terribly alone.

HARKER. Willy! You can't mean that!

WILLY. (*Crossing to* HARKER.) I do mean it! You must pity him, or else commit plain murder. (*She turns to* SEWARD.) To save my soul you must release his, out of mercy, or be as damned by pride as he! (*Turning to* VAN HELSING *and taking his hands.*) You understand, don't you Uncle Abraham?

VAN HELSING. Well, Willy I—

WILLY. He offered you immortality, didn't he? (*The sinister* DRACULA *theme is heard.* WILLY *becomes affected by it, her whole demeanour changes.*) And you've one-upped him! Take care lest you expunge the only mind in the world greater than yours in the guise of decency—

SEWARD. Willy!

WILLY. And salve your precious soul in fastidious humility—by trapping this fabulous monster in your mystical web, using ME as BAIT! AS BAIT! (*She has crossed* D. L. *and breaks into hysterical laughter.*) Delicious ingenue! Only first-class dragons need apply.

HARKER. (*Grabbing her by the arms and spinning her around.*) Willy!

WILLY. Oh bloody paradox! Either way I must end my life with butchers!

HARKER. Stop it! (*He slaps her smartly across the face, then embraces her.*)

SEWARD. You cad, sir! That's uncalled for!

VAN HELSING. Gentlemen, please. Cedric, get her something to help her sleep. (SEWARD *crosses to the side board and pours a glass of brandy.*)

WILLY. (*As* HARKER *seats her by the desk and sits by her on a stool, holding her hands:*) I . . . I'm so sorry. You can't know what it's like, to feel his blood coursing through my veins, to feel myself fading from your world into his—to know that if you fail I will become like him—a murderer for all eternity . . . (SEWARD *has returned with the brandy and holds it out to her.*)

SEWARD. Willy!

WILLY. (*She drinks.*) Uncle Cedric, Uncle Abraham, Jonathan: If everything shouldn't go according to plan, promise me you'll have the courage . . . to do as Godalming has done.

SEWARD. There, there, my girl, no need to dwell on that . . .

HARKER. We have no intention of failing.

VAN HELSING. Willy, try not to think . . .

WILLY. PLEASE . . . Uncle Cedric, have you your Bible?

SEWARD. Why, yes.

WILLY. I want you all to swear on the Bible that if I should become Un-Dead, you will destroy me.

SEWARD. Willy!

VAN HELSING. Cedric— (SEWARD *crosses to the side board and returns with a Bible.* HARKER *rises and the three men place their hands on the Bible.*)

VAN HELSING. I swear.

HARKER. And I swear.

WILLY. Grant me one more request . . . will you read the Order for the Burial of the Dead? Then, whatever happens, I shall be prepared.

HARKER. (*Taking* WILLY's *hands and kneeling in front of her.*) My darling Wilhelmina, I will gladly give up my life for you . . . and if it should turn out otherwise, mine shall be the hand that strikes.

WILLY. I could not wish for better company in which to die.

SEWARD. (*Reading.*) "I am the resurrection and the life, saith the Lord: He that believeth in me, though he were . . ." (*Choked with emotion, he is unable to continue and turns* U. S. VAN HELSING *takes the Bible and continues reading.*)

VAN HELSING. " . . . He that believeth in me, though he were dead, yet shall he live . . . and whosoever liveth and believeth in me, shall never die . . ." (HARKER's *head in her lap*, WILLY *has slumped over him.*)

HARKER. Professor, she's falling asleep. (*He rises, cradling her head in his hands.*)

VAN HELSING. It is a mercy. Help her upstairs, John. Jameson has sealed her windows, so is safe . . . and it is better we do not disturb her with our talk. (HARKER *gathers her up, walking with her* U. S., *a pause and a look to* SEWARD, *and they exit* U. *the stairs.* JAMESON *enters with a tray of sandwiches.*)

SEWARD. (*Taking a sandwich.*) Oh, thank you, Jameson—practically immoral bein' hungry at a time like this, but there it is. Nerves, I guess.

VAN HELSING. Is well you eat. We will have need of strength, I think.

SEWARD. What sort of trouble are you expectin', Abraham?

VAN HELSING. If I only knew! It is almost dawn—he must come soon. Keep your crosses by you, and we may yet prevail.

SEWARD. Jameson, you go down to the dining room and keep an eye out. If you spot anything don't try to deal with it. Doubletime back here, and we'll form the old hollow square. (HARKER *re-enters.*)

JAMESON. Right, sir. (*He exits.*)

SEWARD. (*To* HARKER.) Have a sandwich?

VAN HELSING. We can do nothing now, but wait. (*They all eat the sandwiches in silence. There is a pause.*)

HARKER. (*Seated on the chaise.*) Y' know, there's something odd . . . like being waked by the silence when the foghorn stops . . . it's the dogs! The damn dogs! We haven't heard them howling for some time now.

SEWARD. Damn! You're right! Something's afoot. Think I'll take a look around. Join me, Harker?

HARKER. All right, Professor?

VAN HELSING. Go not too far. You might see to the patients—make sure the attendants are on guard.

SEWARD. Sound idea. (*They exit.* VAN HELSING, *left alone, throws down his sandwich and picks up a crucifix, contemplating it.*)

VAN HELSING. . . . the resurrection and the life . . . (DRACULA's *voice is heard in reverb* V. O.)

DRACULA. (V. O.) I am the resurrection and the life . . . he that believeth in *me*, though he were dead, yet shall he live . . . (*Breathing heavily,* VAN HELSING *grips the crucifix and raises it in trembling hands.*) Whosoever liveth and believeth in *me* shall never die . . .

VAN HELSING. The Lord, GOD, he is king! The LORD GOD, he is King! The Lord God, he is king! (VAN HELSING *rises and crosses to the bookcase.*) My mind, mustn't let him control my mind . . . let me see . . . (*He takes down a book.*) "It was the best of times, it was the worst of times . . ." No, no . . . (*He takes another.*) "Marley was dead to begin with. There could be no doubt whatever about . . ." I don't believe it . . . (*As he is leafing through a third book,* RENFIELD *sneaks in through the French doors. He is carrying a length of rope and his intentions of homicide are clear.* VAN HELSING *catches sight of him out of the corner of his eye and pretends to read.* RENFIELD *advances, raising the rope.* VAN HELSING *steps* D. R. *off the platform.* RENFIELD *advances again, and just as he is about to wrap the rope around* VAN HELSING'S *neck,* VAN HELSING *pretends to see a small animal.*) Pssss. . . . (*He mimes catching it.*) Got tcha! (*He crosses to the desk, cooing to it, and puts it in a desk drawer.*) Oh, that's a fat one. That's a beauty. In you go, my pet. (*Looking up he sees* RENFIELD *and feigns surprise.*) Oh, hello.

RENFIELD. (*Crossing* D. C.) For me?

VAN HELSING. Perhaps later. Mr. Renfield, why not sit down there and have a nice talk with me. Very quietly . . . we don't want to disturb him.

RENFIELD. No . . . (*He sits on the floor, never taking his eyes from the desk drawer.*)

VAN HELSING. You know, I have been thinking about this Life Force theory of yours, Mr. Renfield, and I begin to agree with you . . .

RENFIELD. Good, I knew you'd come 'round eventually . . .

VAN HELSING. But one thing you were clever not to tell—as the power of the body increases, so does the power of the mind—is this not the truth?

RENFIELD. Yes. You grasped it. But don't tell the others. It would only confuse them, they're not prepared for . . . what are you doing? (VAN HELSING *has been adjusting the Lazarus Wheel on the desk.*)

VAN HELSING. Do not be alarmed, Mr. Renfield—I just wanted to show you how I work these things out.

RENFIELD. I'd like that, but . . .

VAN HELSING. Then you must see this wonderful lamp I got from Holland . . .

RENFIELD. It is dangerous?

VAN HELSING. No, no, no. You see, when I must work out a puzzle, I concentrate on this lamp and watch the colors . . . you see how beautiful? (*He*

*has turned out the lights in the room, so that all we
see are the spinning colors of the Lazarus Wheel.)* Just
watch the lights, and you can think about things . . .
difficult things . . . what do the lights remind you of,
Mr. Renfield?

RENFIELD. Eyes . . . his eyes . . . I can . . . No!
You're trying to fool me again. I mustn't speak of him
—not ever . . .

VAN HELSING. But of course you may speak, Mr.
Renfield . . . whatever you wish . . . is fascinating.
Tell me of the eyes you see in the light.

RENFIELD. The eyes . . . the eyes that never close
. . . that watch and wait . . . yes—I see them—now
. . . always.

VAN HELSING. There is another who sees them, is
there not, Mr. Renfield?

RENFIELD. Yes . . . but I mustn't speak of her—
he'll punish me. It is the greatest of mysteries . . .
even I don't understand . . . I can't tell you . . . It
hurts to speak.

VAN HELSING. She is very special, is she not—Miss
Willy . . .

RENFIELD. She is my friend, she never laughed at
poor Renfield . . . she is . . . (*He groans.*) . . . to
be the mother of immortals . . .

VAN HELSING. You mean that with Miss Willy, with
a mortal woman, he would conceive a child?

RENFIELD. She won't be mortal—but . . . but . . .
VAN HELSING. Yes . . . ?
RENFIELD. She must join him of her own free will or
the spell won't work . . .

VAN HELSING. But this is wonderful . . . how did
you come to know this, Renfield?

RENFIELD. He . . . he . . . teaches many things
. . . every night he comes for me. He takes me . . .

my soul flies into the air with him . . . I hover next to him . . . and he whispers in my ear . . . RATS! Hundreds, thousands, millions of rats . . . lives, with years of life in them . . . with eyes blazing red, exactly like his . . . and he tells me—all these will I give you if you will worship me . . . (*We hear* DRACULA's *voice in reverb* V. O.)

DRACULA. (V. O.) Come, my creatures of the night . . . of the dark . . . you shall gnaw English bones at my wedding! Advance before me as I come to claim my own! (*We hear the rats scrabbling toward the stage.*)

JAMESON. (O. S.) RATS! Hundreds of 'em—coming up the lawn—front and back, Dr. Seward! A plague o' rats!

RENFIELD. Lives . . . lives for Renfield . . . Master! You have fulfilled your promise! I am your servant forever!

SEWARD. (*Entering.*) Bloody little devils—we'll have to make a fight of it. Rats, Abraham . . . (*He crosses to get a revolver and a shotgun.* HARKER *and* JAMESON *have also entered.* VAN HELSING *crosses and takes the Lazarus Wheel out of harm's way.* JAMESON *moves to restrain* RENFIELD.)

JAMESON. 'Ere! Come out of it, y' damn fool looney! No! There's too many of 'em for you—

SEWARD. Let him go, there's no time!

RENFIELD. (*Escaping through the French doors.*) The Life Force has come . . . !

JAMESON. They're vicious, sir—what'll we do?

HARKER. Kerosene! You've got to lay down a line of fire!

SEWARD. In the carriage house, Jameson. RUN! (*Grabbing his shotgun, he commences firing on the terrace.*) This'll slow 'em down—Die, you blighters!

Off my lawn, you vicious stinkin' little bastards! (*He exits, firing the gun.*)

HARKER. (*He has rushed to the desk for a gun. He prepares to follow.*) Professor! Keep watch on Willy!

VAN HELSING. (*He catches* HARKER's *arm.*) No, John! Stay by me! It is a ruse—he divides us! The dawn approaches—if he comes, it must be now.

JAMESON. (O. S.) 'Ere's the kerosene, sir!

HARKER. (*Rushing to the doors to watch.*) They're laying down a trail! (*Shouting off to* SEWARD.) Up to the front lawn—quickly!

SEWARD. (O. S.) Light it, Jameson!

JAMESON. (O. S.) Right! 'Ere goes! (VAN HELSING *has been gathering the garlic. He crosses* U. *to* HARKER *and hands him some.*)

VAN HELSING. John, seal this door. When he comes, who knows what he shall attempt? (*He crosses to the windows, sealing them with garlic.*)

(*Ad lib cheer from the lawn.*)

HARKER. They've done it—they've turned them! (*He closes the French doors, sealing them with garlic.*)

VAN HELSING. It is just the prologue—he will be upon us. We must hold him at bay 'til morning.

HARKER. (*Crossing to him.*) And what about tomorrow? We've got to have a plan to destroy him!

VAN HELSING. We must first survive. We must protect Willy from him—from herself.

HARKER. From our stupidity! He'd never have . . .

VAN HELSING. John, Renfield told me something important. Willy must go to him of her own free will if he is to accomplish his plan.

HARKER. Of her own will? Professor, what do you

mean . . . (WILLY *appears on the stairs. She is distraught.*)

WILLY. (*Rushing* D. *the stairs.*) Jonathan, he's coming!

HARKER. (*Crossing to her, trying to hold her.*) Willy —stay upstairs! This is no place for you now!

WILLY. (*Breaking from him.*) He's here . . . all around us . . . I can sense his presence . . .

VAN HELSING. He shall never have you, Willy—we swear it. Take her upstairs, John!

(*During the next speeches the house begins to show the effects of* DRACULA's *spell. We hear wolves, and strange things happen to the lights.* HARKER *goes to* WILLY.)

WILLY. Let me go to him—he'll destroy you all if I don't . . .

HARKER. No! We won't let that happen . . . don't even think!

WILLY. (*Grabbing a stake.*) Then kill me now! There'll be nothing left of me if I have to live another day like this.

HARKER. (*Taking the stake from her.*) Darling, please, I could never . . .

WILLY. But you swore—you all swore!

VAN HELSING. Only should he triumph, Willy, and that he shall never do.

DRACULA. (V. O.) Wil . . hel . . min . . a . . .

(*The French doors burst open and explode; the chandelier explodes, the fireplace explodes, wisps of fog penetrate the room, and the sound begins to reverberate and there is a blackout.*)

VAN HELSING. John—hold Willy! He comes . . .

WILLY. He . . . is . . . everywhere. (*Jonathan is holding her. All three of them are huddled together facing the French doors, awaiting* DRACULA'S *entrance. When the lights restore* DRACULA *is in the* D. R. *corner of the room. The sound of a heartbeat fills the stage. Upon hearing his first words they spin 'round in surprise and fear.*)

DRACULA. So—the game is ended. A pity you will never see the prince that I shall sire upon my bride . . .

VAN HELSING. (*Holding a huge cross in front of him.*) You shall not possess her. She is the child of light.

DRACULA. For all your wisdom, still you do not understand. You say I prey upon the helpless when it is the helpless who rush to me. I do nothing. I simply am. With me, as with all the world, desire is everything . . .

WILLY. (*Reaching for* DRACULA.) My . . . lord . . . (HARKER *can't bear it any longer. He swings* WILLY *aside and lunges at* DRACULA.)

HARKER. You monster!

VAN HELSING. Jonathan, no! (WILLY *screams as* DRACULA *grabs* HARKER *almost in midair and tosses him* S. L. *near the desk.*)

WILLY. Jonathan! (*She rushes to* HARKER.)

DRACULA. Wilhelmina . . . if his life has value for you, I shall spare it. Now . . . turn from these fear-bound mortals and join me in eternity . . . come!

WILLY. (*Rising.*) If you love me, let them live, and I will join you freely.

VAN HELSING. No! Not while God lives! (*He thrusts the cross toward* DRACULA *who is forced back a pace.*) For all your power, still you dread *this!*

DRACULA. (*Starts toward him, forcing himself to*

look at the cross.) My desire . . . is stronger . . . than your faith. Your cross will not defeat me again this night . . .(*He grasps the cross. It explodes with fury.* VAN HELSING *is knocked back, as is* WILLY. DRACULA *screams in pain and releases the cross. He recovers and moves* U. S. *looking at* WILLY.)

DRACULA. Now . . . my queen, know thy lord . . . (*He holds out his hands.)* Come . . . to me. (HARKER *revives to hear this.* WILLY *starts to go to* DRACULA.)

HARKER. WILLY! Resist him!

VAN HELSING. He has no power but that you give him.

HARKER. Think of Helga! You will be queen of graves!

VAN HELSING. He is death! (WILLY *has stopped* C. S., *torn by her impulses.)*

HARKER. (*Rising.)* Shall I be your first victim? My life is yours—will you give it to him—this killer who cowers from the light!

DRACULA. (*Grasps* WILLY'S *wrist, swings her* U. S. *and lunges toward* HARKER, *who grabs a stake to protect himself.* DRACULA *grabs* HARKER'S *throat with one hand, and with the other throws the stake* S. R. *as he strangles* HARKER.) Die, little man! Whimper in your death-cry that you have seen greatness, even as it stopped your foolish tongue!

WILLY. (*Takes the stake and holds it behind her back.)* RELEASE HIM, MY LORD! I . . . AM . . . YOURS!

DRACULA. (*Releases* HARKER *and rushes to her with open arms. She thrusts the stake. There is a still moment, almost an embrace, before she withdraws it.)* Wil . . hel . . mina . . . (*He sinks to his knees.)*

VAN HELSING. Seize him! We finish it! (HARKER

hauls him onto the chaise as VAN HELSING *readies the stake and mallet.* WILLY *is cringing at the doors.)*

DRACULA. My curse upon you for all eternity!

VAN HELSING. (*As he places the stake in position.*) You are dead in your pride for all eternity! (*He strikes, driving the stake into* DRACULA's *heart.* DRACULA *groans and expires.*) Per omnia saecula saeculorum . . .

(*A lone wolf howls.* HARKER *rises and rushes to* WILLY. *She turns and falls into his arms.* SEWARD *and* JAMESON *enter, supporting* RENFIELD.)

SEWARD. (*From o. s.*) Abraham! The rats got to poor Renfield . . . (*Entering and seeing* DRACULA's *bloody corpse.*) Oh my God . . .

VAN HELSING. Is all right, Cedric . . . it is finished.

SEWARD. Willy—is she all right? Is she herself again?

HARKER. She's stronger than any of us, sir. It was she who . . .

WILLY. No, Jonathan, never speak of it—just hold me . . . (*He does.*)

RENFIELD. (*Who has slowly crossed and is kneeling beside* DRACULA.) No life . . . he brought no life . . . only death. What will become of poor Renfield? Why did you betray me, Master? Why . . . ? (*He weeps.*)

VAN HELSING. And so your pride is dust, and your glory the morning of a single madman. Go . . . rest now with the ancients of legend. We are free of you . . . (*He closes* DRACULA's *eyes.* WILLY *and* HARKER *turn to look at the first golden rays of the sun as the music fades* U., *and the lights fade* D.)

CURTAIN

PROPERTY PLOT

Act One, *Preset:*
  Fireplace mantle—box of cigars, clock, matches, ashtray, candlesticks
  Fireplace implements in stand u. s. of fireplace
  Several books on window ledge
  Brandy snifters and sherry glasses on bar cabinet—two decanters inside bar
  Desk: silent butler, ashtray, matches, Bible—stuffed owl on top—several books on shelves inside—gun (practical .32)
  Telephone
  Bell pull
  Mouse on string under chaise
  Wastebasket u. s. of desk

Off Stage L.:
  Feather duster
  Coffee tray with cups, saucers and silver pot
  Metal crash tray
  Jameson's gun
  Renfield's mouse
  Two lanterns
  Straight jacket
  Tray with sandwiches
  Four garlic strands
  Several stakes
  Renfield's rope
  Container of blood
  Clipboard
  The shadow bat
  The swooping bat
  Helga's bloody blouse

Wind machine
Bloody handkerchief
Book for VAN HELSING
Fog machine

Off Stage R.:
Riding crop
Camera with flash equipment and two photoplates
Camera carry case
Folded London Times
Small wooden cross
Hammer
Collapsible stake with attached blood bag
Mallet
Rag for VAN HELSING
GODALMING's top hat and gloves
Exploding cross—unloaded (load for Act III)
Lazarus wheel
"Dial" magazine
Blood capsules
HELGA's notebook and pencil
Cigars
Two boxes—one with books, one with several wooden
  crosses
Wrapping paper and string
Large scissors
Fireplace photograph
Transfusion equipment and bandages
Two afgans
Small throw pillow
Neck chains with silver crosses
Doctor's bag
Raisins
Containers of blood

COSTUME PLOT

Act One

SEWARD:
Matching light brown vest and cuffed pants
Dark brown tweed jacket
White shirt with collar
Green tie
Brown wingtip shoes

JAMESON:
Brown pants and vest
White shirt
Black tie
Black shoes
Carmel sweater

VAN HELSING:
Long gray coat
Gray pants and vest
White striped shirt with collar
Tie and suspenders
Brown shoes

HELGA:
Tweed suit (long skirt and long jacket)
Gray tie shoes
White lace blouse with small neck tie

GODALMING:
Beige riding pants
Brown boots
White ascoted shirt
Light brown jacket

RENFIELD:
　Matching light blue-gray jersey pants and shirt
　Brown suspenders
　Black felt crepe-sole shoes
　Small pouch attached to pants

HARKER:
　Dark blue vested suit
　White shirt with collar
　Red tie
　Black wing-tip shoes
　Motorist's cap
　Motorist's overcoat

WILHELMINA:
　Turquoise and beige lace tea gown
　Beige slippers

DRACULA:
　Long double-breasted velvet coat—black
　Black velvet pants
　Short black boots
　White ascoted shirt with jeweled brooch
　Floor length silk lined black velvet cape with black
　　lamb's wool high collar

ACT TWO

SEWARD:
　Mourning suit and vest
　Black shoes and tie

GODALMING:
　Mourning suit and vest
　Black shoes and tie
　Gray spats

JAMESON: Same—Act One

WILHELMINA:
  Peach satin lace trimmed nightgown
  Peach velvet lace trimmed dressing gown robe

HARKER: Same except—
  no jacket
  no vest
  beige sweater vest—change tie

VAN HELSING: Same—change shirt and tie

HELGA: Long low-cut lavender burial gown—light
  flowing material

RENFIELD: Same

DRACULA: Same—no coat for second scene
  Shirt with long puff sleeves (no buttons)

ACT THREE

All same except—
  SEWARD—change back to Act One but no tie

  VAN HELSING—no coat

  DRACULA—special coat and padding for staking

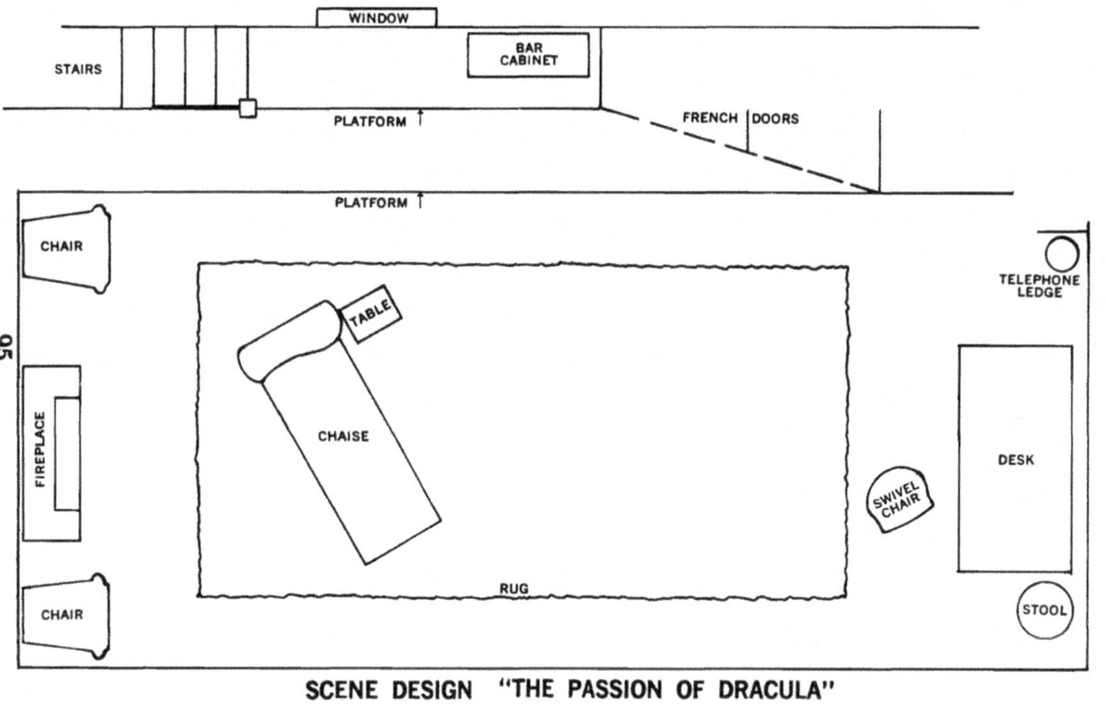

SCENE DESIGN "THE PASSION OF DRACULA"

MUSIC USE NOTE

Licensees are solely responsible for obtaining formal written permission from copyright owners to use copyrighted music in the performance of this play and are strongly cautioned to do so. If no such permission is obtained by the licensee, then the licensee must use only original music that the licensee owns and controls. Licensees are solely responsible and liable for all music clearances and shall indemnify the copyright owners of the play(s) and their licensing agent, Samuel French, against any costs, expenses, losses and liabilities arising from the use of music by licensees. Please contact the appropriate music licensing authority in your territory for the rights to any incidental music.

IMPORTANT BILLING AND CREDIT REQUIREMENTS

If you have obtained performance rights to this title, please refer to your licensing agreement for important billing and credit requirements.